THE
GHOSTLY TRIO

By NANCY WOOLLCOTT SMITH

Illustrated by Charles Beck

SCHOLASTIC BOOK SERVICES
NEW YORK • TORONTO • LONDON • AUCKLAND • SYDNEY • TOKYO

TO SUNDY

Copyright 1954 by Nancy Woolcott Smith. This edition is published by Scholastic Book Services, a division of Scholastic Magazines, Inc., by arrangement with Coward-McCann, Inc.

12th printing .... February 1972

Printed in the U.S.A.

CONTENTS

1. JACKIE

BEFORE Jackie was even awake she could feel the oddness of the new brace on her teeth. She ran her tongue experimentally along the bright gold band and rolled over. She burrowed her tousled red head in the pillow and sighed luxuriously, a sad, muffled sort of sigh.

Being sad was really just a game today. Whenever she wanted, Jackie could turn over again and feel the gladness pouring in. Whenever she wanted, she could open her eyes and see the sun splashing through the window with a special sparkle that was meant for holidays.

This morning Jackie, who was eleven and whose whole name was Jacqueline Lee Murray, had an important engagement. It was an engagement to go on an expedition and a picnic even though it was still really winter. Already she could smell the coffee-and-bacon smell of breakfast time. But it was fun to stretch out and think about the two new boys who had become her friends and of the holiday that lay ahead.

Two days of Teachers' Convention, two days of week end, and then came Monday. But not the ordinary gloomy Monday, for this one came on February 22nd, Washington's Birthday. That made five whole days of fun and play with Dick and Sam. It was wonderful not to envy her sister Miriam and the secret clubs she had with the giggling older girls at school.

A few minutes later Jackie, in rolled-up jeans and floppy plaid shirt, bounced down the stairs, two daring steps at a time. Her heavy jacket was tied around her waist and the top of her hair had been brushed almost smooth. But underneath, it was still tangled and snarled. Jackie tried to run her fingers through it with little success. She hoped the family wouldn't notice. It was already after nine and there was no time to lose.

In the dining room Miriam was helping Mother, grown-up fashion, the way she always did on holidays. When Jackie and Miriam were little they had played together always. But now that Miriam was almost fourteen, she no longer liked to romp in the fields and play Indians and cowboys. Now Miriam played only with the giggling older girls at school, and Jackie was not asked to join them.

Jackie sat down quietly in her own seat, adjusting her chair so that the little crack in the table was exactly in front of her nose. That was the way she must always sit —she had forgotten just why. Miriam tossed her shiny yellow hair back over her shoulder and sipped self-consciously at her coffee, a special treat she was allowed on holidays because she was so old.

Jackie smiled to herself. She liked milk better anyway. And now she had her own secrets, her own friends. She was not even curious about Miriam and her club. She began eating her cold cereal in big spoonfuls

6

without looking at Miriam. It crunched in her mouth. noisy and defiant.

"Good morning, Jacqueline!" Mother came out of the kitchen, her cheeks flushed from the heat of the stove, her old blue apron wrapped snugly around her good black dress. Probably she was going to town.

"Morning." Jackie hurriedly drained her milk.

"How does it feel, dear?" Mrs. Murray asked. She drew her chair up to the table and smiled sympathetically at Jackie.

Jackie remembered the brace. She pressed her tongue against the inside of her teeth. They felt like somebody else's and not like her own at all.

"Terrible," she answered with feeling. "Simply terrible."

"I never made a fuss like that when—" Miriam began but Mrs. Murray hushed her.

"Why must I suffer like this?" Jackie asked dramatically, taking advantage of the sudden silence.

"I suppose," Miriam snorted, "that you'd like your teeth to be all crooked when you get big and go to parties and dances and things."

Jackie didn't answer. She knew now with all the sureness she ever knew anything that she would never care if her teeth stuck out, as long as they were strong and white. She would never care about those silly parties and dances that seemed to mean so much to Mim.

"Why must I suffer like this?" Jackie repeated, her mouth full of bacon.

"Perhaps you better change and come with me," her

7

mother suggested. "I'm going shopping and can let you off at Dr. Brown's. He said to come back if it bothered you."

Jackie glanced at the clock. It was almost ten. Dick and Sam might not wait if she were late. She wasn't that important.

"No. No thanks. It'll be all right, honest." Jackie pushed away from the table.

"Well, you certainly changed your mind in a hurry," Miriam teased as she put an extra-big spoonful of sugar in her coffee.

Miriam probably didn't like coffee anyway, Jackie reflected. She probably just drank it to be grown up as she did so many things. Ignoring her, Jackie untied her jacket sleeves knotted about her waist and thrust her arms into them. But her mother stood between her and the door.

"Now, Jacqueline." Mrs. Murray's voice was pleasant but it called for an answer. "You'd better tell me where you're going."

Jackie took a deep breath. "If you must know, out to the lake for a picnic."

"Goodness," said her mother, just as Jackie had expected. "It's scarcely picnic weather. Besides I don't know what there is for you to take."

"My friends are bringing lunch," Jackie answered. "I'll take it next time."

"I," Miriam spoke importantly, "have a place to picnic that isn't outside and not in anyone's house either."

8

"Where?" Jackie forgot she wasn't interested in Miriam's doings any more.

"Wouldn't you like to know!" Miriam smiled one of her mysterious, annoying smiles. "It's our club secret."

"Pooh," retorted Jackie, the beginning of an idea stirring in her head. "You aren't the only one who can have a club." She turned toward the door, throwing a questioning glance back at her mother.

"Be home well before dark," Mrs. Murray answered her look, which meant, of course, "All right, you may go."

"Thanks!" Jackie rushed from the room.

"Jacqueline, Jacqueline Lee," Miriam called after her, her voice half childish, half grown up. "You can't go out before you make your bed."

"Let her alone, dear," Jackie heard her mother's low voice. "Anything to make her forget that brace. I can't bear to have it bother her."

As Jackie fumbled with the outside door, she felt a sudden wave of tenderness for her mother. After all, she did care, at least a little, about the foolish brace. She ran back into the dining room and gave her mother a bear-like squeeze. Carefully ignoring Miriam, she whispered in her mother's ear, "It's better now already."

Again she bolted for the door. Just before it banged behind her, she could hear Miriam's voice raised for her benefit.

"Well, I never! Well, I never! Such a brat!"

2. THE GHOSTLY TRIO

THE AIR was crisp and cold and clear, but the sun already felt warm on the top of Jackie's bare red head. Anyway, she reflected as she wheeled her bicycle out of the garage, she hadn't been sent upstairs to comb it. Coasting happily down the drive she noticed how blue the sky was above the bare branches of the maples. There weren't many big trees around Kingsville any more and not many big old houses like theirs either. They were all being made into apartments or torn down to make room for the rows of little city-like houses that were going up all over town.

It wasn't until the second row of brick houses was finished in the field across the Pike from Jackie's house that Sammy and Dick had moved into Number Twenty-eight. And now Jackie was glad of the new houses and the two new boys they had brought. She stopped at the end of the drive beside the mailbox to wait for them. Far above her head she could see the swelling buds on the top branches of the maples dark against the morning sky. In other years Jackie had written little verses about the spring, but boys might laugh at things like that.

She could see them coming, Dick first, speeding toward her, his lanky body erect on the seat. But Sam followed slowly. His bicycle zigzagged aimlessly back and forth across the road. His plump shoulders slouched over the handle bars.

Dick skidded to a halt at Jackie's side. She was careful not to jump lest he should laugh at her. Sam coasted slowly up behind him, the sunlight flashing on his dark-rimmed glasses. Jackie's eyes turned toward the bulging paper bag each boy carried in his bicycle basket. They hadn't forgot to bring the food.

"You're late," accused Jackie as if she herself had not just arrived.

"Couldn't get Sam away from that book." Dick laughed teasingly. He was a tall slim boy of twelve, half a head taller than Jackie.

"Studying again!" Jackie screwed up her freckled nose. "And on a holiday, too!"

"Wasn't studying. I was reading." Sam scowled, his face round and dark as Dick's was fair and narrow, as serious as Dick's was gay. They didn't look like brothers.

"Reading or studying. What's the diff?" Without waiting for an answer, Dick started off along the Pike.

"Plenty." Sam turned toward Jackie. "I was reading a story. A ghost story. All about—"

"Let's go." Afraid of losing Dick, Jackie shoved off after him.

Sam followed slowly, his untold story spinning tantalizingly in his head.

When they reached the lake they left their bikes among the pines that lined the shore. Carrying their heavy bags of lunch, they walked softly on beneath the thick green branches. There was a wonderful Christmasy fragrance and a gentle bouncy crunch to the needles that lay drying in a thick carpet on the ground. No one felt like rushing now. They stopped often, sometimes to skip small flat stones across the water, sometimes just to stare at the sparkling ripples of the lake.

Only a little way offshore a tiny hump of an island stuck above the surface. To Jackie its small grove of trees looked as deep and magical as a jungle. It seemed so near, yet so far away. She had a fleeting vision of herself at the helm of a small boat sailing the boys across the water to explore.

"If we only had a boat," sighed Sam, his eyes following Jackie's to the island.

"No boating allowed," Jackie answered crisply. It bothered her that Sam so often seemed to guess her secret thoughts. "Can't you even read?" She pointed crossly to a weather-beaten sign tacked on a tree.

Sam squinted into the sunlight and read with gloomy eyes:

NOTICE TO TRESPASSERS
No Hunting with Dog or Gun
No Fishing, Swimming, Skating or Boating
Extinguish All Fires
Do Not Throw Refuse in the Lake
Violators Will Be Prosecuted the Full Extent
of the Law

Kingsville Bureau of Water Supply

"Yikes." Sam shook his head bitterly. "There isn't anything they'll let you do."

"And they don't even use it for drinking much any more, Daddy says," Jackie added. "Not since they built that new dam upcountry."

"What's the diff if they don't let you swim or anything?" Sam turned broodingly toward the water. It looked inviting in spite of the silvery crust of ice around the edge.

"Say!" Dick's voice was high with the excitement of discovery. "Will you look over there." He pointed down the lake where the great stone towers of an old house loomed up behind the pines.

"Oh," exclaimed Jackie. "Ruins. There used to be houses here. Before the dam was built. Years and years ago."

"Bet they're haunted." Sam stared with dreamy eyes.

"Come on, let's explore." Dick was off again in quick strides along the edge of the lake.

"And eat," muttered Jackie, whose stomach was beginning to grumble hollowly. She stepped out briskly after Dick.

As usual, Dick was the first to arrive. "Jeepers," he called back to them. "It's like a castle with thick stone walls, but it hasn't any roof."

"And I thought there might be ghosts," Sam sighed.

"What of it?" retorted Dick. "It's got a wonderful, enormous fireplace."

"But look at the sunlight." Sam wrinkled his pug nose disdainfully.

13

Dick flicked his fingers, which usually meant he had a good idea. "We can have a fire right in the fireplace."

Jackie helped Sam unpack the lunch. They lined up wieners, mustard, milk, cups, cookies and toffee in a straight row while Dick set about gathering wood and laying the fire. He placed twigs wigwam-fashion over a handful of dry leaves. After laying on larger pieces, he lit the leaves casually with a single flick of a match. But as he worked he couldn't resist an occasional over-the-shoulder glance at the others. He liked to have an audience and wanted to be sure they were noticing. Then, with a flourish, he took out a shiny new penknife and was off again in search of sticks—long fresh green ones for roasting wieners.

Together Jackie and Sam watched the bright flames lick upward around the damp wood. Soon it began to steam and then to crackle.

"Time for chow. Time for chow."

Dick charged back holding before him three long sticks, the forked ends sharpened to neat points. He tossed Sam and Jackie each a stick. Each speared a wiener and held it sizzling over the crackling flames. The great room, roofless as it was, soon filled with a mouth-watering aroma as driblets of grease oozed out and hissed into the flames.

One by one the wieners were placed on rolls and their charred bodies were spread with golden mustard. Even as they ate, each roasted a second and then a third. Jackie handed around the paper cups and passed the milk. There were bits of butter floating on top of it from all the churning and joggling on the trip. Sam tossed Jackie and Dick each an apple, opened a box of gingersnaps, and divided up the toffee into three neat piles.

Jackie studied her pile wistfully. Chewy candy was forbidden because it might loosen the tight gold bands that held her braces. She put a piece tentatively in her mouth just to suck it. On either side of her Dick and Sam worked their jaws with noisy vigor. For a long time nobody spoke.

"Oh boy," Jackie broke the silence, her eyes roving around the shell-like interior of the castle. "Miriam can't get ahead of us." Her mouth was still bulging with her first toffee although the boys were already working on their last.

"What you mean?" asked Sam between chews.

"She says she has a place to picnic that isn't outdoors or in anyone's house either," Jackie explained sucking cautiously as she spoke. "She told me this morning, just to tease. But that's what we got too. This isn't exactly *out* or *in*."

"Where you suppose she goes?" Dick asked curiously.

"Oh, this is much better than any place of hers, I bet." Jackie dismissed Miriam with a shrug. "Even if she does have an old secret club."

"It's all right for picnics," Sam admitted grudgingly. "But the house in that book I was reading—"

"Always bringing books home from the library," Dick scoffed.

But now, toasting their feet before the fire, seemed a

good time for Sam's tale. "Go on." Jackie turned toward Sam. "Tell us about it."

Sam needed no urging. Staring fixedly at the fire as if he were reading his story from the flickering glow, he began:

"Well, there were three boys who found an old, old house. Older than this, I guess, only it had a roof and doors and windows all boarded up, you see. But these kids managed to break in. Inside, it was all dark and gloomy, see, with big cobwebs and spooky corners. Not like this," he added with a glance at the sunny wind-swept walls around them.

"These boys explored every room in the house except one at the end of a dark passage in the cellar. Whenever they came close to that room, a low kind of moaning noise would scare them away, and once they saw a misty white sort of thing slide down the passage and disappear into that room, right through the door."

"A ghost," whispered Dick forgetting he was not interested in Sam's book.

"I bet they were imagining." Jackie felt a chill run up her spine, partly from the story and partly because the sun had dropped below the castle walls. "Daddy says there aren't any ghosts, not really."

"Did they ever get in that room?" Dick turned his other shoulder toward the heat of the fire. Although their fronts were toasting warm, a winter breeze played chillingly on their backs.

"Yes," Sam went on hurriedly now. "They went back with lanterns to scare away the ghosts and found a secret panel in the wall. Behind the panel was an old, old chest full of ancient coins and precious stones."

"Jeepers!" Dick took a long breath. He stood up stiffly and began to collect odds and ends of paper napkins and crusts of bread, and toss them into the fire. "I'd like to find a house like that."

"So would I." Sam felt the statement quite a safe one.

Dick filled an empty milk container with water from the lake and poured it, hissing, onto the fire. "Tomorrow," he said blinking from the smoke, "we'll go exploring some more. Maybe we can find a whole house to explore. Since Sam's so anxious to see a ghost," he added teasingly.

"I only want to find out if there *are* any really," Sam explained seriously.

"Well," said Dick with a last satisfied look at the steaming black ashes, "today's only Thursday. That still leaves us four days to find one."

"I know what," said Jackie. As she followed Dick out into the open, she remembered the idea Miriam had given her at breakfast. "Let's have a club like Miriam's, only much better. We can call it the Trio," she added, for she didn't want there to be any other members besides Sam and Dick and, of course, herself.

"And the club will be for exploring deserted houses and looking for Sam's ghosts," said Dick, who always wanted to be doing things.

"And treasure," added Jackie as if she really thought they'd find one.

"I'll get a notebook and write down the club rules

and all our findings," Sam announced happily. "You come over in the morning and we'll get started."

"Do you have to *write?*" groaned Dick, who was taking long strides back along the lake the way they had come.

But Sam was thinking. He followed behind without bothering to answer.

When they reached the place where they had left the bicycles, the sun already had dipped low over the lake. It sent a streak of warm yellow light across the icy ripples. Jackie noticed her island again, now black against the setting sun, so close and yet, without a boat, so far away.

Each threw a final stone across the water before starting reluctantly for home, taking with them in their clothes and hair the smell of wieners and wood smoke.

"We'll call ourselves the Ghostly Trio," Sam announced as they parted at Jackie's driveway.

"The Ghostly Trio!" Jackie whispered the words after Sam. They had an exciting, magic ring.

3. A FALSE LEAD

THE SUN was already high in the east. A strong breeze caught the tops of the big maples, splashing their dark dancing shadows over the Murrays' rambling white house. The front door opened and closed again with a resounding bang as Jackie came out and dashed down the drive between the trees. With a quick glance to right and left she trotted across the Pike and down the new white road on the other side. It had a sign swinging over it:

WILDWOOD: THE FINEST HOMES IN
KINGSVILLE

This was foolish as there was nothing either wild or wooded about the straight, bare, treeless streets or rows of small city-like houses.

Number Twenty-eight once had seemed as strange as all the others, but now it was almost like home to Jackie. She ran up the white wooden steps and pressed the bell three times, a signal that it was she. Inside she could hear a chimes resounding through the house— not the angry buzz of their own bell at home, but a peal of musical notes. "Da dee da. Da dee da. Da dee da." Three times. Clear and beautiful.

"Come on up. Come on up." Loud and impatient, Dick called to her from the little room he shared with Sam. Since their mother worked she was seldom there to let Jackie in. Jackie pushed open the door, which was never locked, and went bounding up the newly varnished stairs to join the boys.

Instead of beds the boys had bunks, one above the other, covered with gay spreads. Against the opposite wall was a shiny maple desk, and at the desk Sam sat writing, his chubby shoulders hunched over a new black notebook. There was only one desk for the two boys but there were never any fights. Dick just hated to sit still.

"Hi," said Jackie to Sam's back. "What have you got?"

Sam drew one more careful block letter on the cover of the notebook before he held it up for Sam and Jackie to see. A tingle of anticipation went through Jackie as she read the square neat lettering:

GHOSTLY TRIO

Sam opened the notebook, his pencil poised above the first blank page. "Its aims and purpose," he suggested.

Jackie nodded approval. At least it sounded important.

"All right." Dick shuffled impatiently. "What *are* the aims and purpose of this club?"

Jackie looked at Sam. Sam looked at Jackie.

"To find some—some ghosts," Jackie suggested uncertainly. When Sam had told them his story before the dying fire in the old ruined house, it had seemed a logical and daring enterprise. But now in the boys' sunlit room it did sound rather silly.

"But where can we look?" Sam said, his stubby fingers playing thoughtfully with the pencil.

"Let's look around the lake again!" Dick suggested. His long legs were itching to be off.

Jackie shook her head. "I was telling Daddy about our picnic place, and he says it's the only ruin left standing near the lake."

"But we have to find an *old* house." Dick took his jacket from the closet. "Otherwise it wouldn't be haunted."

"Around here everything is new." Jackie glanced gloomily out of the window at the rows of little raw houses.

"And a *deserted* one," Sam added. "Ghosts don't like a lot of people."

"Dad says there are so many people in Kingsville now that they live in anything. Even in trailers," Jackie sighed.

"Jeepers!" Dick snapped his fingers as if he had the problem solved. "*I* know someone who knows all about houses." He thrust his arms decisively into the sleeves of his jacket.

"Who, Dick? Who?" Every time Dick had an idea it was something that called for action. Like Dick, Jackie hated staying in. There was enough of that at school.

"Mr. Blake, the building man. My pal." Dick's left

hand clasped his right to indicate the closeness of the friendship. Dick had pals all over Kingsville, although he'd lived there just a month. Mr. Danbridge in the hardware store, the policeman down on Main Street, Dr. Miland, the village druggist—he counted all his friends.

"Come on." Dick slapped Sam across the back. "Let's go ask Mr. Blake. He'd know if there were any deserted houses around."

For a moment Sam stared fondly at his notebook. Then rolling it up reluctantly, he wedged it into his hip pocket. He tucked the pencil in with it and went slowly after the others, down the stairs and out into the windy sunshine.

Dick led the way toward Mr. Blake's office, the builder's shack in the far field where the last of the new houses were still going up. A narrow gangplank of old boards led over the newly turned earth to the door. On it someone had painted in wiggly black letters:

Wildwood Construction Company
Private
Keep Out

Ignoring the sign, Dick pushed the door open. Hesitantly Jackie and Sam followed him. Mr. Blake, a huge, muscular man, his collar open, his shirt sleeves rolled up, his hat on the back of his head, sat at his desk talking to several workmen who stood about the potbellied stove.

"Well, young ones," he boomed jovially at the Trio, "what's on your mind?"

Jackie gulped and turned toward Dick for help. Sam was so busy studying the charts and blueprints on the wall he seemed scarcely to have heard.

"It's like this, Mr. Blake," Dick explained, reddening as all the other men in the room stopped their talk to stare at him. "Know if there are any old houses around here? Deserted ones, I mean."

"Oh, so you're looking for spooks, are you?" Mr. Blake's laugh filled the room.

"Oh no!" Dick contradicted hastily. "Just looking around."

"I see," Mr. Blake answered, winking at the workmen. "My business is new houses, but when I was surveying I did hear about one old one."

"Where? Tell us where!" clamored Jackie, forgetting to be shy.

" 'Bout a mile from here. Over on what was the old King estate. Only part that wasn't sold to those Garden Manor people and torn down when they put up their subdivision."

"I remember King's Manor." Jackie sounded pleased and important. Of the Trio she alone had seen the old place as it used to be. "But I didn't know there was an old house left. Is that empty?" she asked, making the "empty" sound too important.

"Yes, Reds." Mr. Blake ignored Jackie's frown of disapproval at the hated nickname. "That's been empty for nearly a year, ever since—"

He hesitated.

"Since what?" Sam's round dreamy face focused to

attention. He was hoping for something to put in his notebook.

"On second thought," Mr. Blake said, speedily and unreasonably changing his mind, his voice louder than ever, as if to erase what he'd said before, "perhaps that isn't such a good haunt. Someone probably living there now."

The Ghostly Trio stared at him in puzzled disappointment.

"But I'll tell you," Mr. Blake boomed gaily. "I know one that's empty for sure and old too."

"Where?" Jackie's green eyes flashed hopefully. Sam reached for his notebook.

"Well now, Reds, let me see," Mr. Blake answered. "Back behind the blackberry thicket where the grading stops. Right in the meadow. There's a fine little old deserted house there. Made to order. Fits all specifications." He rubbed his big hands together in a pleased-with-himself sort of way.

"You mean that old tool shed or whatever it is?" Dick's face reflected the scorn in his voice.

Mr. Blake nodded. He stopped rubbing his hands.

"We've passed that hundreds of times." Jackie wrinkled up her nose in disgust. "That's not really a house at all."

"But it's very, very old." Mr. Blake looked so crushed that Jackie was afraid she had hurt his feelings. "It's the oldest thing around these parts."

"Guess it is." Dick turned toward the door. Mr. Blake didn't know as much about houses as they did.

"I'll tell you something else," Mr. Blake added, as if sorry to disappoint them. "A crazy man used to live there, eat and sleep and all. So you see, it really is a house."

"A crazy man?" Sam's eyes grew wide. "Did he *die* there?"

"Don't know for sure," Mr. Blake hedged. "He hasn't been around since I've been on this job."

"Oh." Sam's hand closed over his notebook. At least there was something to record.

"Thanks, Mr. Blake." Dick threw open the door, eager for the bright crisp air after the stuffy smoke-filled room. "Sorry to bother you."

"No bother at all," Mr. Blake answered genially. "But you boys be careful. 'Specially with your girl friend along. And don't go fooling around that shack after dark," he added lowering his voice to an ominous, full-bodied whisper.

"Okay and thanks. Thanks." Without bothering with good-byes the Ghostly Trio rushed out again into the sunshine.

"Why didn't we ever think of that?" Jackie asked breathlessly as they ran past the skeleton frames of the last new houses, on toward the undeveloped waste of marshy field and briar.

For the first time they did not stop to watch the workmen, to see what progress had been made since the day before.

"We didn't know about the crazy man," Sam panted as he clogged along behind Dick and Jackie down into the thicket. "He makes all the difference in the world."

As the twining briars and tall winter-dry grass almost closed out the sight of Wildwood and its people, the abandoned meadow seemed suddenly eerie and far away from the rest of the world. Yet the path the trio followed was more trampled and used than Jackie remembered it.

"Do you suppose that crazy man has come back?" Jackie asked, half hoping, half afraid.

"Course not," Dick answered loudly. But it seemed to Jackie that he had been wondering too. For reassurance she turned to Sam. He was busy fishing the notebook from his pocket.

"Trail well-worn," Sam muttered as he wrote.

"Maybe he goes back and forth a lot to get water and things." Jackie glanced uneasily over her shoulder.

"Look!" Dick had already disappeared around a particularly thick clump of briars. His voice came back to them high with excitement.

Jackie hurried after him. Sammy, stuffing the notebook into his pocket, panted along behind, his glasses bouncing precariously.

There was the shack they had passed so often without a thought. But today it was different. The three stopped motionless, staring uneasily. The old, cracked windows stared back at them, oddly clean and unfamiliar. Behind them hung incongruous bright new curtains of flowered chintz. There was a shiny padlock on the warped door, and a bucket of water stood on the ground beside it.

"He *does* go back and forth for water." Jackie gazed incredulously at the bucket.

"Jiminy!" Sam's eyes were saucerlike. "Let's go!"

Dick and Jackie shook their heads, each a little frightened and each more than a little pleased. From beyond the meadow came the steady hammering from the new houses and the patient chug of a tractor grading the bumpy roads. A bird chirruped in the thicket close by, and all around unseen things were moving, thawing out after the long winter. Spring was on the way and the world seemed far too friendly to let them be afraid.

"Do you suppose he's in there?" Jackie managed a hoarse whisper, trying to get back a little of the fear and delicious excitement.

"Sh—" Dick cocked an ear. "Somebody's coming."

In the silence that followed, they could hear the snap of a twig, the swish of a branch on the trail behind them.

"Into the bushes." Dick's voice was tense. "Duck, so he can't see us."

The Trio ducked for the thicket. Scarcely breathing they crouched in silence, their eyes fixed on the trail.

There was a snatch of song, clear and high, and then a giggle. Around the bushes appeared two disappointingly familiar figures—Miriam and her chum, Janet Parker.

"Pst, Jackie, that's your sister, isn't it?" Dick whispered, nudging Jackie's arm.

Jackie nodded glumly. She noticed that Miriam was carrying a heavy basket over her arm as if she were

27

headed some place in particular. Janet carried a big cardboard sign. Even from her hiding place Jackie could make out the tall slim letters:

KINGSVILLE SOCIAL CLUB
FOR MEMBERS ONLY
KEEP OFF

Jackie watched the intruders, and she muttered a little secret spell that would make them pass the shack and go on to something else. But it didn't work. Miriam put her basket down beside the door. Pulling a key from a pocket of her carefully creased gray flannel slacks, she fitted it easily into the padlock. The door swung open and the two girls disappeared within as if the place belonged to them.

"That settles it," Jackie hissed angrily. "Those two would be enough to frighten away the toughest ghosts."

"I think Mr. Blake was fooling us." Sam began thinking back over their talk with him. "You could tell he was just trying to give it a build-up."

"But it does make a peachy clubhouse," Jackie sighed. "Wish we'd thought of it first."

"But why," brooded Sam as they crawled back unnoticed through the bushes and went slowly home along the trail, "why should Mr. Blake have told us all that junk about a crazy man?"

"Dunno." The slim adventure over, Dick was not one to worry about the "why" of things.

"I think," Sam chewed thoughtfully on his pencil, "I think he did it to make us forget the other house, the one he started to tell us about and didn't. He switched—

"Why, Sam!" Jackie turned to stare at him in admiration. "That's right. He did change the subject in a hurry. He was telling us about an old house left on the King place and then just stopped and never finished."

For once Dick looked baffled. "Don't even know where he meant."

"The King place was sold to a building company," Jackie explained, pleased at knowing something Dick didn't. "They tore it down before you ever came to Kingsville. I didn't know any part was left. Anyway, that's where they built those ugly new houses called Garden Manor."

"Oh, Garden Manor!" Dick snapped his fingers as if everything was clear. "That's less than a mile, over there across the meadow."

"But those are all *new* houses," Sam protested.

"Dr. Miland at the drugstore might know if there's really an old one left." Jackie grinned at her own bright idea. "Just before it was torn down he took pictures of the King place and gave them to the historical room at the library. Daddy says he's the only one who cares about old landmarks and history."

"History!" Dick scoffed. "But okay. Dr. Miland's my pal anyway. Let's go to the drugstore right after lunch. We can get cones and then ask Doc about that house —real casual-like. We'll show Old Man Blake he can't fool us."

"We'll show him," Jackie and Sam agreed in unison as the three trudged hungrily home to lunch.

4. HOUSE IN THE PINES

MIRIAM wasn't home for lunch. Mother said she was visiting, but Jackie guessed she was picnicking in her new clubhouse. A little wave of sadness swept over Jackie. She was remembering how hurt and miserable she used to feel when Miriam did things without her. But now Jackie had her own friends, her own adventures, and she was almost glad that Miriam wasn't home, because Mother let her have her lunch quickly, sitting on the kitchen stool. A peanut butter sandwich, milk, and a chocolate bar. Then she was off again.

By the time Jackie had wheeled her bicycle out of the garage, Sam and Dick were waiting on theirs at the end of the drive. Side by side they coasted down the Pike to town.

The drugstore was a small crowded room heavy with the mixed and fascinating smell of medicine and perfume and nickel candy bars. With easy assurance Dick led the way to the counter. The three climbed onto stools, where they perched twirling, waiting for service.

"Be with you. Just a sec," Dr. Miland called from the prescription counter at the back of the store.

Jackie spun herself around toward the fountain to ponder over the long selection of flavors posted on the

big mirror. For a second her reflection stared bac̶̶̶
her. Cheeks red from the windy trip down the hill.
Tight red curls tossed wildly above the heart-shaped
face. It wasn't a bad face, with its big green eyes and
turned-up nose, even though the freckles were more
noticeable than usual. She smiled experimentally. The
reflection smiled back. If it weren't for the gold band
that flashed on her teeth . . .

"Hi ya, Doc."

With a guilty start Jackie turned as Dick greeted the
druggist. She didn't want to seem like Miriam, staring
in every mirror that came her way.

Dr. Miland, his face round and pink and scrubbed,
stood behind the soda fountain. The overhead light was
reflected in the shine of his bald head, like a moon on a
glassy sea.

"Well, Dicky boy," he exclaimed happily, "how goes
it? And Jacqueline! My, but you're getting to be a big
girl."

Jackie winced. He had greeted Dick as an equal. But
to her he spoke as he would to a little girl, a little girl
he had known since her mother had pushed her around
in a baby carriage. It would be wonderful to be like
Sam and Dick and live in a new place where no one
remembered what you were ten years ago.

"What will it be?" Dr. Miland asked briskly.

"Cone, please," Jackie answered. "Butter pecan."

"Strawberry." Dick licked his lips in anticipation.

"Ah—ah—ah—chocolate." Sam had been too busy
with his notebook to decide before.

, know the old King place?" Dick asked
he accepted his cone.

it!" The druggist paused in his work with a
smile. "Oldest home in Kingsville. Criminal to
y it."

"Was it all destroyed?"

"Yes. Wicked to tear down old landmarks for these
new developments."

"But we heard," Jackie tried to sound indifferent,
"that there was still a house left. On the King place, I
mean."

"Only the old tenant's house hidden away back on
the knoll." The druggist handed them their cones.

"Oh," said Jackie, "you mean way up in the pine-
woods? I didn't know that was part of the King place."

"Used to be," Dr. Miland answered. "That will be
thirty cents, my friends."

"Thanks." The Trio clinked their dimes onto the
counter and wandered off, sucking thoughtfully on
their cones.

"That must be where it is. The house Mr. Blake
started to tell us about and didn't." Jackie broke into an
excited skip as the big glass door swung shut behind
them. "Let's go see if it's really deserted."

"Okay," Dick agreed. "But let's take our bikes home
and walk across the meadow. That's the best way to the
knoll."

As the three set off on foot across the meadow the
sunshine was chilled by sharp gusts of wind that

whipped challengingly into their faces. Fast dark
sent shadows skimming across the winter-brown
meadow grass. To the west the lake lay gray and sullen,
flecked with silver whitecaps.

At the far end of the meadow another path wound
up a wooded slope back of the new brick houses of
Garden Manor. Even in winter, with the trees bare and
the ground brown and stubbled, the knoll had an inviting explorable look. There were so few woodsy places
left near Kingsville now.

"This must be the way." As usual Dick was in the
lead. "Doc said 'back on the knoll.'"

"Oh, Dick," Jackie sniffed happily at the damp rooty
smell beneath the trees, "when we were little, Mim and
I used to walk here with Mother. There used to be lots
of wonderful old houses where that ugly Garden Manor
is now. There was a big stone mansion and a gatehouse
and stable and a whole row of little shacks."

"Gosh, Jackie, did they really have slaves in Mary-
land?" Sam stopped with interest.

"Come on." Dick started up the knoll. "We're interested in old houses that *haven't* been torn down."

On the crest of the knoll, in a grove of ancient pines,
they found it. Surrounded by a thickly tangled hedge
was a small gray house snuggled down beneath the pine
boughs. Its porch was rickety, its windows shuttered.
The old chimney was crumbling and smokeless, and
suddenly they knew they had found adventure.

"Camouflage," whispered Sam. "It's as gray as the
tree trunks."

house." Dick stared approvingly. "Win-
ey, porch and—oh, does it look old!"
serted," added Jackie.

rab green shutters, almost black with age,
to whisper a warning to keep away, and at the
same time an invitation to pry them loose to see what
lay behind. Altogether it was almost as spooky as the
house in Sammy's story. Now suddenly Jackie wished
they had never come.

"What's the matter, Jacqueline? Aren't you going
in?" Sam always called her "Jacqueline" when he was
bothered or disturbed.

"Go right ahead, sir." With a mock bow Jackie mo-
tioned to a small gap in the hedge. But Sam suddenly
was preoccupied. Busily he reached for his notebook.

Dick gave them a suspicious look and marched
boldly through the opening. Jackie meant to follow him,
but instead she found herself standing close to Sam.
Together they watched Dick from behind the hedge.

Almost inaudible sounds seemed to surround the
house. Sounds something like a whispered sigh, something like a muffled moan. But then, when they listened
again, there was nothing, nothing but the swishing of
the pine boughs in the wind.

Nervously running her tongue along the ridge of her
brace, Jackie kept her eyes on Dick as he moved cautiously across the creaking, sagging porch. The door-
knob rattled noisily as he tried it. In spite of herself
Jackie felt relieved to find the door didn't open. But
Dick, his courage mounting, went along the length of

34

the porch and disappeared around the corne
house.

Uncertainly Jackie glanced at Sammy. With painful
slowness he was writing the words *Door Locked* in his
precious notebook. But Jackie had no excuse to keep her
standing there, not even a notebook. With sudden determination she hurried after Dick.

Around the corner of the house a shutter hung on one
hinge. Lopsided, it dangled from a solitary window.
Dick, who stood contemplating the window, turned to
give Jackie an appraising glance.

"Not scared?"

"Are you?" Jackie hedged.

As if in answer, Dick put both hands on the window
and pushed up. Jackie drew back involuntarily as she
saw it give. With mixed delight and horror she watched,
as little by little Dick raised the window until an open
space lay between them and the dark room inside. Like
a magnet it drew Jackie toward it. With beating heart
she poked her head inside.

From above, there was an explosive bang. Alarmingly
it resounded through the still dark house. A ghostly
breath of foul air poured out through the window,
touching Jackie's face and making goose-pimples rise
up at the roots of her red hair. Blindly she turned and
ran, Dick close on her heels. Ahead of them Sam, who
had only just reached the porch, stumbled in retreat
across the yard.

"Dick, what was it?" Jackie whispered when they
were safe on the other side of the hedge.

...utter banging in the wind," Dick an-
...ly. "Why did you go and run at a little
...ked crossly, ignoring the fact that he had

...'t the noise," Jackie replied uncertainly. "It
wa—it was—" She paused for lack of words and looked
anxiously at Dick. But he was not laughing. He understood. It was the breath of evil-smelling air that had
brought the chills to their hearts, for Dick had smelled
it too.

"Come on." Dick shook himself as if to cast off the
fear.

Jackie nodded. She glanced at Sam. He was busy
writing again, careful not to meet their eyes, and Jackie
knew he was afraid.

5. AN UNEXPLAINED DEPARTURE

SOMEHOW Jackie got back again across the yard, across the creaky porch to where the window stood open and waiting as if to swallow them. Jackie held her breath and forced her unwilling head into the blackness. Dick stood close beside her. But Sam, chewing anxiously at his pencil, hung back when he got far enough to see.

At first Jackie was conscious of nothing except the dank air that poured steadily out toward the daylight as if it were fanned by some mysterious force. Remembering how she had jumped before, she was careful not to draw back. Deliberately she squinted into the gloomy room, trying to make out what lay beyond the window sill.

"It's got furniture still." Apprehensively Jackie looked at the boys.

Dick nodded, for he had seen it too. Sam reached for his notebook without bothering to see for himself.

"Go on in." Dick gave Jackie a nudge from behind.

Jackie swung her leg over the window sill and dropped to the floor on the other side. The chill of the musty air closed about her. Glancing back she saw Dick, and finally Sam, climb in behind her, their bodies silhouetted against the wintery light of the afternoon out-

ey came to stand beside her, their
cutting through the ghostly quiet of
ackie it seemed that she herself didn't

their eyes adjusted, the dark dwindled.
'I.. ..as small, far too small to hold comfortably
a table, . broken-down sofa and an odd assortment of
chairs.

"Perhaps," Dick suggested, "it was a very big family." He muffled a giggle.

Angrily Jackie realized she had been clinging to his
arm. Clutching like a frightened child without even
knowing it. She pulled away and took a brave independent step across the room, where she could see a pale
streak of light under a closed door.

"It won't turn," Jackie whispered as she fiddled with
the catch.

Dick hurried to her side. "It's a latch, not a knob.
You have to lift. Like in old-time houses."

"Oh, now I know!" All at once Jackie understood
about the smell. That bittersweetish, strangely familiar
smell that filled the air, penetrating through dampness
and dust. That was like Grandmother's country house.
It was the smell of kerosene lamps that clung to the
walls, the floor, the ceiling, and not the smell of ghosts
at all. But before she had time to explain, Dick succeeded in opening the door. On tiptoe they entered the
kitchen.

A pale grayish light came through the one shuttered
window, throwing a peculiar striped pattern on the

dusty floor. Under the window was a clumsy sink with a funny little hand pump growing out of one end of it. His eyes lighting up, Dick grabbed the handle and began working it energetically.

"Maybe it's got to be primed," Sam suggested, his fears momentarily forgotten. Both boys leaned over the old pump, inspecting it uselessly.

Jackie, who did not even know what "primed" meant, turned away to look about the kitchen. Her eyes, now adjusted to the gloom, were beginning to see things, little things they hadn't noticed before. What they saw made them open very wide indeed.

"Look." Her voice was uneasy. "Dick, look!"

The boys left the pump and hurried over to where Jackie was standing beside the big kitchen table. They saw the old blue plates, dark with layers of dust, that were set about it. They noticed too the dried, crumbling bits of matter that had once been food on the plates. They saw the caked, decayed stuff in the bottom of the pitcher that might once have been milk, and the mildewed tablecloth.

"They left things just like that," Jackie gasped, "right in the middle of dinner!"

"Or maybe breakfast." But the thing Sam tried to make sound like a laugh rattled strangely in his throat.

"People just don't go off like that." Jackie looked furtively over her shoulder as if the explanation might be lurking in the far corner of the room.

"That's right," Dick whispered wisely. "When we moved to Kingsville from the country, we packed all the dishes in a barrel and took our last meal in a diner."

"Of course. That's what everybody does," said Jackie, who had always lived in the same house.

In awe they stared at the disordered table, trying to piece together the story it had to tell. The wind had started up again. They could hear it whistling through the pines and around the old chimney. A shutter banged against the open window in the living room, but the Ghostly Trio stood very still, being careful not to jump.

"What made them do it?" Jackie asked in a voice that didn't sound like hers at all.

"It must have been something," Sam answered huskily. "Something about this house," he added edging backward toward the door. "A ghost, maybe."

"There aren't any ghosts. Not really," Jackie protested, but without conviction.

"How about in Sam's book?" Dick reminded her.

"But that was just a story." Jackie ran her tongue excitedly along her brace. "Now we've found something real. Much worse than any ghost." She looked about, her eyes wide and frightened in the gloom. "We must find out what it was. What it was that made them leave."

"Maybe there was something here." Sam bit nervously on his pencil. "Something someone else wanted, like the hidden jewels in that book."

"What do you mean?" Realistically Dick glanced around the shabby room. "Anyway, why would that make anybody leave?"

"Because the man who knew about the treasure did

things—horrible things to frighten the owners away." Sam edged out of the kitchen toward the safety of the open window.

Just then the pump handle that Dick had left poised in mid-air dropped slowly, with an eerie squeaking groan that shattered the thick silence all about them. Standing in the kitchen Dick and Jackie saw and knew what it was. But even knowing did not keep their hearts from jumping up again.

Sam, near the open living room window where he couldn't see, tumbled backward over the sill. Frantically he ran down the hill toward home.

" 'Fraid cat," Jackie tried to call, but the words only formed on her lips. Without reason she stumbled after Sam. Dick, his long skinny legs covering two steps in one, caught up to Jackie as she dashed out through the hedge.

"We can come back again tomorrow," he announced bravely as the three went thankfully home across the familiar meadow. Jackie nodded. Even Sam made no protest. Tomorrow was a long way off.

"Let's stop by Mim's club," Jackie suggested as they reached the far edge of the meadow. "We can spy on them."

They walked Indian fashion, one after the other, with long slinky steps, each with a hand raised before his eyes. Now back in their own familiar world they felt tough and confident again.

"Hark!" Jackie ordered just before they turned the bend by the shack. "Listen!"

The high sound of girls' voices came to them through the gusty air.

"Poor things, that's all the haunted house they can find." Jackie smiled with satisfaction. "Ours is a real Mystery House."

"Let's give it a little spice for them," Dick suggested condescendingly. He leaned over and loosened a stone from the icy mud. The others followed suit. On tiptoes they rounded the bend and hid behind a clump of bushes within a few feet of the Kingsville Social Club. They could hear the girls inside talking and giggling as they always did.

"One—two—three!" whispered Dick, taking aim.

He hurled his stone. It banged with fury against the old shack. As the noise echoed away across the meadow, Sammy's stone hit the old boards with a grand resounding bang. Jackie's missed by yards.

The Ghostly Trio turned and ducked back around the bend. Behind them they could hear the screams and high, excited giggles of Miriam and her friends. Perhaps they thought that ghosts had visited their club.

Feeling happy and quite superior, the Ghostly Trio went on their way.

6. FORBIDDEN ROOM

EVERYTHING looked bright as Jackie woke the next morning. A sprinkling of snow almost covered the dark, stubbled field.

"It *would* snow with spring almost here," Jackie muttered crossly. But deep inside she felt a secret gladness that fresh snow always made her feel.

When she reached Wildwood the boys were waiting, throwing snowballs at each other in the street. Together they hurried off toward the deserted house on the pine-clad knoll. Along the path they noticed footprints of a man and a dog that had come that way before them.

"Probably just a hunter," figured Dick, but Sam wrote down "footprints" just in case.

Once more before the Mystery House, they stood staring in at the little gap in the hedge. The footprints of the man and dog went straight ahead along the path.

"Wonderful thing, snow." Sam smiled knowingly. "You can see no one's been through the hedge since it fell." He recorded this in his notebook.

The house looked bleak and dismal even in the brightness of the morning. But there was no whispering in the pines today. The snow that sifted down through the tangled branches touched the snow on the ground without a sound. Dick glared at Sam, as if he and his writing were to blame for keeping them standing there. With sudden determination Dick turned and led the other two through the hedge.

The side window was still half open, just as they had left it in their flight the day before. This time no one stopped to whiff the damp ghostly air or to listen for noises from within.

The kitchen was lighter than it had been the afternoon before. The morning sun hit full against the shutters, sifting through the slats in dusty beams upon the disordered room.

"Just think," Jackie murmured, "whoever lived here must have just up and left, right in the middle of supper."

"Still think it was breakfast." Sam shuffled in the kitchen door, a hand deep in his hip pocket.

"No," Jackie retorted with conviction. "It must have been supper. Really, this house isn't scary in the morning."

Dick nodded. "No, it isn't a bit scary in the morning," he repeated loudly, but his eyes, quick and alert, darted about the room. "The trouble must have happened at night, after the sun went down."

"We must look for clues." Sam pulled his hand out of his pocket, and with it the notebook. "What were they having to eat?"

"Silly, you can't tell that." Jackie approached the table gingerly. "All the food is dried to dust."

"Here's an old ball," Dick observed as he poked around.

Sam licked his pencil. "Children in family," he muttered as he wrote. He did not move away from the door.

Jackie felt brave as she followed Dick about the room, looking for clues. "Look, there's a huge old raincoat on that hook, and here's a cake of soap and a hammer by the sink."

"Everyone has soap and hammers." Sam frowned disapprovingly. "We've got to look for *unusual* signs." He explored the room, but only with his eyes. His feet seemed rooted in the doorway. "Where does that door go?"

"Go and look for yourself," Jackie answered, but Sam's head bent suddenly over his notes again.

It was Dick who tried the door at the far end of the kitchen. It opened with a grating squeak and a cloud of dust. Behind it steep dark stairs led up into a cobwebbed gloom. Jackie and Dick started up the stairs together, warily, one halting step at a time.

"Aren't you coming, Sam?" Jackie raised her voice to reassure herself. Looking back she could see Sam standing in the kitchen below, a gleam of light sparkling on his glasses.

"Soon as I catch up on my notes," Sam answered evasively.

In the darkness Jackie's boot groped about exploringly before she realized she and Dick had reached the top. On either side a dim thread of light ran along the floor.

"Must be doors," Jackie observed as Dick found the latch and pushed one quickly open.

Together they stared into a small room. There was nothing in it but four iron cots wedged closely in a row. Indeed there was space for nothing else.

"A fine place to sleep!" Jackie felt a wave of pity for the children she imagined sleeping in this room. Like paupers in a storybook. "No wonder no one lives here!"

"But," protested Dick, "why should they have left in such a hurry? We washed all our dishes and put them into barrels before—"

"Yes, yes," Jackie interrupted, "I know."

"I'll try the other door." Hurt, Dick moved away. "Hey," his voice rose excitedly. "This one's bolted, way at the top. Maybe to keep kids out."

"Oh!" Jackie gasped in happy consternation, the thoughts of treasure flashing back. "Perhaps Sam was right. Perhaps someone did chase the family away so they could get it. And that's why the room is locked."

"Well," Dick spoke with false assurance, "there's only one way to find out." Standing on tiptoe his fingers just reached the bolt. "It's stuck," he announced, "and it's too high for me to get a good grip."

"Oh, bother," said Jackie feeling both disappointed and relieved.

"You try." Dick turned to Jackie. "I can hold you up."

"N-n-no." Jackie looked uneasily at the bolt. "Maybe we better leave it alone."

"What's going on up there?" Sam's voice came irresolutely up the dark stairs.

"Bring up the hammer. It's by the sink," Dick called down to him as nonchalantly as if he were asking for

46

something out of his own toolbox. But Jackie detected a quaver in his voice.

"Oh, Dick, let's not—" She broke off, wanting him to stop, wanting him to go on.

"Sissy." Dick snapped his fingers in Jackie's face.

Even Sammy's courage seemed to revive a little with something to do. He crept up the stairs, hammer in hand, and gave it to Dick. Then he retreated again, but only halfway down.

Jackie held her breath as Dick raised the hammer. He tapped the bolt with sharp quick blows. The metallic clangs resounded accusingly through the empty house.

His lips pursed, Dick inspected the rusty bolt. He gripped the hammer tighter, his face set and determined. Jackie ground her teeth in agitation, but she was too excited to notice how it made the brace hurt her.

As Dick raised his hammer and aimed a blow, he heard Sam on the stairs. His voice between a scream and a groan came hoarsely up to them.

"Stop! Stop!"

It was too late. Dick couldn't stop. The hammer hit the end of the bolt. The bolt slipped back. With a kind of gasp the door sprung partly open. Dick and Jackie stood cowering at their own audacity, catching their breath before they approached.

In that short second of silence they heard what Sam had heard before. A long low whistle pierced the air. Dick's hammer thudded to the floor. But the door quivered on its hinge, leaving an open space between them and the forbidden room that gaped accusingly.

7. ESCAPE

THERE WAS a pattering of feet around the house and then again the whistle, long and low.

"Better hide," Dick whispered as Jackie looked around in panic. Where in a house without a closet could anyone hide?

From outside came the sharp growl of a small dog just below the window and a man's voice calling him.

"Here Sport, here Sport," deep and gruff. "Nobody lives there. Come on, fellow."

They listened thankfully to the footsteps moving off, and a moment later the yipping of a dog behind them. Dick gave a loud sigh and turned again toward the open door.

The room beyond it was small and gloomy, even smaller than the one across the hall. It was furnished with only a cot, a desk, and a broken chair. The desk, a huge old-fashioned one, was littered with dust-covered papers and a long array of dusty, dried-up ink bottles. Two pipes lay side by side in a grimy bowl, and the place seemed still to smell of ink and tobacco.

"The study," Jackie sighed. Her mind raced back to her father's study at home, the big swivel chair she liked to spin in, the firelight rosy on the book-lined walls. "What an awful place to study."

Dick nodded and the two stood staring disappointedly at the desk.

"But why did they lock it?" Jackie puzzled.

In answer Dick began to pace the room. Occasionally his hand went down experimentally, feeling for a loose board along the molding. Once or twice he tapped the wall. Jackie knew he was thinking about the treasure in Sam's book. As if such a thing could really happen!

As she followed Dick around, Jackie's eyes fell upon an old calendar hanging high above the desk. She raised it hopefully. Dust filtered down into her eyes. Impatiently she dabbed at them with the sleeve of her parka.

Beneath the calendar the wall was two shades lighter, a square, mysterious patch.

"Dick!"

He hurried to her side. Together they felt the wall where the calendar had been. Dick tapped it with his hammer. There was no sliding panel, no secret door. Only a square of old plaster a little less dirty than the other plaster on the wall.

"Oh, Dick," Jackie muttered, "and I thought—"

"Aw grow up, Jackie," he answered crossly as if he himself had had no hopes.

"Well, what's in here?" Sam's voice startled them. He stood in the doorway, having finally got up his courage to follow them that far.

"Nothing," Jackie yawned. "Nothing but a desk and a lot of old papers, and it's the last room. Let's go."

"Desk? Papers?" Sam repeated with rising interest. "Let me see."

Jackie led the way back to the desk. Sam, forgetting his fears, followed her. He inhaled a lungful of cold damp air and blew it out again over the littered desk. Dust rose in a dirty cloud and then settled again over the papers.

"Looks like a lot of wastepaper to me," Jackie sighed, "and a couple of old checkbooks too." She touched them gingerly with the tip of her finger. "One from the Kingsville National and a couple from some city banks. Nothing interesting."

"Yeah," Dick agreed, "and there's some more junk." He indicated a cardboard box that evidently had served as a wastebasket. It was overflowing with dirty crumpled papers. "Let's go."

But Sam was not to be hurried. Brushing Dick aside, he pulled up the broken chair and sat cautiously on the edge of it.

His eyes greedy, he gazed at the old desk before him the way an ordinary boy might gaze at a turkey dinner before digging in. Then slowly and deliberately he took a yellowed sheet from the pile, adjusted his glasses, and leaned over to examine his prize.

There was a sudden bark, close beneath the window now. Off in the woods a man's voice answered. "What is it, fellow? You smell something back there?"

They could hear the crunch and crackle of underbrush as someone came pushing through it. Without thinking Sam crumpled the paper into a tight ball and stuffed it into his pocket. The Ghostly Trio stared at each other in confusion. Did the little dog know what his master did not know—that there was someone in the Mystery House?

"Well, I'll be busted," the man's voice broke out angrily. "Someone's gone and forced a window."

"Come on," Dick whispered urgently. "Let's get out of here."

Jackie turned and tumbled wildly down the dark stairs, Dick breathless beside her. But Sam was not so terrorized as to leave everything behind. With one swoop he gathered up a handful of papers and tucked them quickly inside his jacket. For once he wasn't the first to run.

Dick and Jackie stumbled through the kitchen. But at the living room door they skidded to a stop. Dark against the brightness of the snow, a huge figure stood outside their open window. They could see a giant of a man with a wide-brimmed hat pulled low over his face and great hunched shoulders blocking their escape.

Dick stared at Jackie. Jackie stared at Dick. Blank fright was in both faces. But Sam, who had crept softly down the stairs behind them, was busy at the kitchen door. Slowly he pulled back the rusty bolt. At the creak of the opening door, Dick and Jackie turned. Behind Sam they ran out across the yard and down the hill, feet and hearts pounding in unison.

In their panic the Trio scarcely noticed the yipping of the dog close on their heels. They were far more aware of the man's voice. Angry and threatening, it called to them to stop. He might have been the monster who frightened the owners away. But no one turned back to have a good look.

8. SAMMY'S LOOT

"YOU'RE late again. And look at that mud!" Miriam looked disapprovingly at Jackie as she thumped panting into the house.

With deliberate rudeness Jackie turned her back on her sister. She pulled off her boots, squidging up her toes so that the shoes wouldn't come with them. It used to make her miserable when Miriam started talking like a fussy parent instead of the pal she used to be. But now, bursting as she was with her own importance and excitement, Jackie didn't care. Her heart still thudded from the narrow escape from the Mystery House, but not unpleasantly now. With a contented sigh of relief she wiggled out of her parka, leaving it in a dark heap in the middle of the floor. Miriam swooped down upon it, clucking like an outraged hen, and bore it haughtily off toward the closet. It was easy to tell that this was one of her grown-up days.

It was Saturday and Father was home for lunch. There could be no quick snack on the kitchen stool today. Daddy liked everyone to sit down and be sociable. Miriam trotted importantly back and forth from dining room to kitchen, her new shoes clicking noisily. She wore one of Mother's aprons over her good dress, and her golden hair was carefully set with bobby pins. As on other recent Saturdays she was probably going to the movies with the "girls," as she called her friends, pronouncing girls with a special emphasis.

Jackie surveyed Miriam's shoes with distaste. They had little inch-high heels, a first step toward grown-up ones. "They wouldn't be much good for running," she said meaningfully.

"What do you mean?" Miriam looked at her sharply, a suspicious glint in her eyes.

Remembering yesterday, Jackie only giggled. There were bigger mysteries on her mind than any old deserted shack.

"Daddy," she asked casually as they settled down to lunch, "does anyone live in the tenant's house on the King place?"

"Old Mason?" her father asked vaguely. "Wonder where I put those pruning shears."

"Yes, Mason." Now at least Jackie knew his name. "Does he still live in the tenant's house?"

"Guess he left about a year ago. The sun's warm— things are drying up in a hurry."

"Left?" Jackie's eyes were wide. "Why did he leave? Daddy, why did he leave?" Conscious of the urgency of her voice, Jackie took a big forkful of potatoes to hide her interest. Did her father know the answer to the interrupted meal? Did he know the secret of the forbidden room? The reason for the prowling man and snooping dog?

"Oh," Jackie's father answered casually, "he got into a bit of trouble around here."

"What, Daddy? Daddy, what kind of trouble?" Jackie's voice came out high and shrill.

"Gerald!" Mother rang a warning from the other end of the table. Jackie knew what that meant.

"Oh, nothing," her father answered abruptly.

No amount of questioning would do any good now. There was something that Mother didn't want her to know. Jackie finished lunch without thinking what she ate, the words "Mason" and "trouble" circling in her head. There was a real human mystery to their Mystery House. Not just their own imagining. Not like thinking up crazy men in a deserted shack or treasure in a shabby cottage.

With an almost inaudible "excuse me," Jackie pushed away from the table. Dragging on her parka, which Miriam had tucked carefully away in the very darkest corner of the closet, Jackie hurried off to Wildwood and the boys.

Dick was waiting for her outside, restlessly tossing a soft ball into the air. Now that the snow was almost gone, he had apparently decided it was spring.

"I've got something to tell you," Jackie announced.

"We've got something to show you."

"What's up?"

"Shh, come on in and see." Dick led the way to the door. "Better wipe your feet," he instructed. "This is Mom's day off and she's cleaning house."

Jackie looked down at her muddy shoes uneasily. Then she wiggled out of them and left them on the doorstep. In her socks she tiptoed after Dick.

The boys' mother, looking fat and comfortable in a floppy house dress, was on her hands and knees waxing the living room floor. She smiled and waved at Jackie. Jackie waved back as she hurried up the shining stairs. The whole house seemed to smell of wax and furniture polish and new wood and varnish.

Sam, as usual, was sitting at the desk. He turned to grin at Jackie, his eyes sparkling behind his glasses. On the desk in front of him lay a strange collection of soiled, crumpled papers. They had all been smoothed out and arranged in some kind of order. A little bronze elephant here, a stone there, a hammer and Dick's basketball trophy served to hold down the curling edges.

Jackie stared for a moment before she understood. They were the papers, the bits of useless scrap that Sam had snatched from the Mystery House desk.

"Oh." Jackie's face lit up as she recognized them. "Those papers. I'd forgotten. What do they say?"

"Nothing, if you ask me." Dick shrugged but his eyes were excited. "Sam's trying to make them mean something. You know Sam," he added with a condescending laugh.

"*Do* they mean anything?" Jackie said to Sam's back as she hurried over to the desk.

"Shh." Sam scowled. "I'm solving the puzzle of why they ran away from that house."

"Maybe there isn't really a puzzle." But the gloom in Dick's voice was forced. He looked as if he thought there really were a big one.

"No one would just up and leave." Sam sucked his

55

pencil. "Not unless something pretty bad had happened."

"That's right," Jackie agreed. "Now I'll tell you what I know," she added impressively.

"What?"

"Daddy told me—" she began, to give her story extra weight.

"You didn't tell him we'd broken in, did you?" Dick asked crossly.

"Of course not, silly." Jackie made a face at him. "I just asked him some questions about the house, real casual-like, to see why those people ran away."

"Why?" Dick and Sam stared waiting for her answer.

"The man got into some kind of trouble and *that's* why!"

"What kind of trouble?" Eagerly the boys leaned toward her.

Jackie gulped. "I don't know," she admitted lamely. She felt she had let them down. After all the build-up, there was so little to tell. But immediately her face brightened. "Maybe the law was after him. I think Daddy would have told me but Mother stopped him. He just shut up about the house the way Mr. Blake did. There's something they sure don't want us to know."

"I think," Sam began, his voice low and confidential, "that this must be the trouble." He turned back to the desk, indicating the papers with a grand sweeping gesture. Jackie too turned toward the desk. She had almost forgotten the papers in the excitement of telling what she had learned. Her eyes dropped to the nearest one, the one with the elephant holding it down. It was dirty and creased, and the letters, in faded blue ink, were sprawly and grown up and hard to read. But even at a glance Jackie could tell there were only two words on the sheet. These repeated themselves again and again all the way from the top to the bottom.

"Johnson Danbridge," Jackie made it out at last. Her lips formed the words. "Johnson Danbridge, Johnson Danbridge, Johnson Danbridge—Oh, Sam," she broke off, "how silly!"

Sam shook his dark head wisely and adjusted his glasses. Without answering he pointed a pudgy thumb at another paper. It, too, was worn and crumpled, but

the typewriting on it was easy to read. The letterhead at the top was in clear bold print: DANBRIDGE & CO., MAIN STREET, KINGSVILLE.

"Dear Mr. King," Jackie read rapidly. "The enclosed is an estimate of the supplies you mention in your inquiry of the 6th. Please communicate with me as soon as possible to enable us to make an early delivery. Yours truly, Johnson Danbridge."

"So what?" Dick climbed to his favorite perch on the top bunk. "Nothing funny about ordering something from Danbridge's. Everybody does that."

"But why," Jackie's forehead puckered, "why should Mr. King's letter be there in the caretaker's house? And why should Mr. Danbridge have signed his name all those extra times besides signing on the letter?"

"But *did* he?" Sam scowled. "That's what I'm trying to figure out."

"What are the other papers?" Jackie's eyes scanned the desk.

"Just names again, like the first. As if someone were *practicing*." Sam gathered them into a neat pile and handed it to Jackie.

Jackie looked at the top paper. As Sam had said, it was just a name. In bold old-fashioned letters it repeated itself the entire length of the page.

"G° Washington," said Jackie, reading. "That's a funny name, Go." She looked at it again. "Maybe it isn't Go," she decided. "Maybe that circle isn't meant to be an 'o' but a fancy kind of period hanging in the air. That would make it just the initial 'G.' "

"G. Washington." Sammy nodded approval.

"Never heard of him. But I know who Mr. Danbridge is," Jackie boasted. "Been in his store with Daddy lots of times."

"Sure," said Sam. "So have we. Now look at the next one."

"S. S. Miland, S. S. Miland, S. S. Miland," Jackie read. "Sounds familiar."

"Course." Dick peered down from his perch above their heads. "He's *Dr.* Miland at the store. But look at the last one," he cried excitedly.

Jackie looked. "Howard S. Blake, Howard S. Blake, Howard S. Blake," she read shaking her head in bewilderment. In spite of the oldness of the paper, the ink had remained a vivid green. "Gosh," she sighed, remembering back to the littered Mystery House desk, "there were a lot of ink bottles. But I still don't see what's so keen about a bunch of silly names."

"Howard S. Blake. Don't you know who that is?" Sam's round face looked as severe and teacherlike as he could make it.

Jackie thought, first on one leg, then on the other. "You mean *Mr.* Blake?" she squealed. "*Our* Mr. Blake?"

"Sure." Dick squirmed impatiently on his perch. "Sure. His name is Howard."

"Now, if we only had a letter from Mr. Blake or Doc with their signature on it," Sam began in his lecturer's voice, "then we could tell if that caretaker guy really was copying their names same as he was copying Mr. Danbridge's."

"But why should he?" Jackie questioned.

Sam gave her a grateful smile. Resting his elbows on the desk, his chin in his hands, he was ready for a long explanation. "Now listen, Jackie—"

"I've got it!" Dick came sliding down over the side of the bunk.

"Got what?" Sam groaned. Dick had been sitting still three whole minutes. It was useless to try and explain things now.

"We'll get Mr. Blake to sign his name for us and then see if that man copied his writing the way you said." Dick picked up his jacket from the floor.

"But he'll get suspicious. We never asked him to sign before," the cautious Sam protested. "And we don't want him to know about our getting those papers from the house."

"I know." Dick pulled on his jacket. "He can sign in my autograph book. That will make it look on the up and up."

"But—" This time it was Jackie's turn to protest. She herself had given Dick the book several weeks ago on his twelfth birthday. "That's meant for ballplayers and movie stars and famous people."

"I know." Dick reddened. "But we never do seem to meet any movie stars or things, and we might as well use the book for something."

"Okay," Jackie agreed. "It's a shame to waste it, and Mr. Blake is an important man, at least around here."

At the door Jackie pushed back into her shoes, and together they ran out of the house and down to the end of the sidewalk. Teetering on the strip of narrow boards that led over the wet ground, they hurried through the unpainted door of Mr. Blake's office without taking time to think how foolish their request might sound.

" 'Morning, Mr. Blake," Dick greeted him cheerfully, forgetting that it was afternoon.

"Hello there, young fellow. How's the spook hunt coming along?" Mr. Blake asked lustily. "See you got your sweetheart with you again."

Jackie could feel her face turn warm and pink, way up to the roots of her red hair. She wasn't Dick's sweetheart. She wasn't anybody's sweetheart. She was just—just part of the Ghostly Trio. But one couldn't explain this to Mr. Blake.

"And how's the young student today?" Jocularly Mr. Blake turned toward Sam. "Your dad's been telling me about you. Says you'll go to college someday. Bet you're sorry Monday's Washington's Birthday and no nice school for you."

Sammy stared at him sullenly.

"Well, what can I do for you people today?" Mr. Blake pushed his chair back from his desk and assumed a more serious tone.

"Oh—oh—ah—" Dick started uncomfortably.

"Well—" began Sam fidgeting with his glasses.

"You see—" Jackie groped for words. "I mean—er—that is, we thought that er—that you might sign our autograph book."

"Sign your autograph book?" Mr. Blake's voice was no less loud for being puzzled.

61

The Ghostly Trio nodded uneasily.

"We're collecting autographs of all the important people we can," Jackie blurted out. "We want you to be our first," she added, remembering the book was still quite blank.

It sounded silly because Mr. Blake was not an important person at all, not anywhere except in Wildwood. But Mr. Blake himself didn't seem to find it so. Smiling graciously he reached for his pen. Taking a bottle of ink from the drawer, he elaborately filled it.

"Green ink," cried Sam, his eyes large behind his glasses.

"Never saw green ink before?" Mr. Blake boomed. "That's my specialty. Wouldn't be my writing without green ink."

Unconscious of the quick glance that passed among the Trio, Mr. Blake wrote his name, big and bold and green, from one side of the little page to the other.

Their thanks were fast and confused. Mr. Blake no sooner had lifted his telltale pen from the paper than Dick grabbed the autograph book. Out they rushed into the damp springlike air. Over the wooden gangplank. Down the new white sidewalk. Back to Number Twenty-eight and the papers from the Mystery House.

9. STRANGE EVIDENCE

"IT'S THE SAME, all right, ink and all," Dick announced as he opened up the autograph book Mr. Blake had signed beside Sam's old paper. "Real copies of Mr. Blake's name all over this piece of scrap. Now what do you make of that?" He turned impatiently to Sam, who was studying the two writings in his own deliberate way.

Jackie too turned toward Sam, waiting to hear what he would say.

"Listen." Sam lowered his voice impressively. "That caretaker man—what did your father say his name was?"

"Mason, I think."

"Mason must have found a letter or something from Mr. Blake, like the Danbridge letter, in the Kings' old house before it was torn down. If he was caretaker, it would have been easy for him to steal old letters with signatures," he added significantly.

Jackie and Dick nodded silently and waited for Sam to go on.

"He wasn't a real thief, exactly," Sam continued, spacing his words with maddening slowness. "He was something much more clever." He paused to be sure they were listening.

Even Dick stood quiet and attentive. Only his fingers moved restlessly, but he was careful not to snap them.

"The man who ran away from the Mystery House must have been a forger," Sam concluded. "That's why he had to leave the house so quickly. He probably tried to forge a check or something. They were after him. That's the trouble your father meant."

"Oh, Sam," Jackie whispered, full of admiration. "There were a lot of old checkbooks there. You're a regular detective!"

"Gee willigers!" Dick let go with the loudest snap of the fingers he had yet accomplished. "Wonder if that's right."

"Well, here's the evidence." Sam indicated the desk. "Someone was copying their signatures. Mr. Blake's, Mr. Danbridge's and Doc Miland's. All people we know, too, except that Mr. Washington." He settled back to the desk like a man with a pile of work before him.

"What's the use of sitting here?" Dick reached for the door. "Let's go ask Doc if he was forged. No sense stewing over these old papers."

"No," Sam retorted with unusual decisiveness. "The one *I* want to find out about is this Washington guy."

"We don't even know where he lives," Dick objected.

"We could look in the phone book." That was a keen idea. Jackie felt like a real detective.

"He's not in it," Sam answered unexpectedly. "I already looked before you came."

"Oh, did you?"

"I looked for Go Washington and a George too, just

in case it was meant to be a dot after the 'G' instead of an 'o'."

"George Washington," Dick scoffed. "Just because it's near his birthday! That 'G' could just as well stand for Gordon."

Sam frowned and chewed at his pencil, a sure sign he was getting set to do some heavy thinking.

"Come on." Dick swatted him across the back. "Let's go talk to Doc and see if that guy really got his dough. I could use a popsicle, too."

"No. I want to check on this Mr. Washington first."

Jackie looked at Sam with interest. He hardly ever said "no" to Dick.

"What's the good of Mr. Washington when we don't even know who he is or where he lives?" Still wearing his jacket, Dick shuffled in the doorway eager to be off.

"I can find out at the library," Sam answered. "That is, if he lives around here."

"Library!" Dick gave a snort of contempt. "Always going to the library."

"They got a book there," Sam went on, turning toward Jackie. "Tells everybody's name and address in all of Kingsville and the city too, even people without a phone."

"Would it take long?" Jackie asked uneasily.

"No," Sam promised, "just a sec. We can stop by on the way to Miland's."

"Okay, but I don't see why we couldn't find out about the forger from Doc instead of some old Mr. Washington we don't even know," Dick agreed reluctantly as they hurried out to get their bikes. "And I'm not going to stay. That library gives me the willies."

"How do you know when you've never been?" Sam asked pointedly. Dick only made a face.

When they reached the library, Jackie and Dick held back uncertainly, letting Sam lead the way. To the north, south, east and west were book-lined rooms, each marked with its own particular label: Fiction, Science, History, Biography, Reference.

Dick cast Jackie a bewildered glance. But Sam seemed as much at home in the library as Dick had been in Mr. Blake's office. He went boldly up to a big desk where the librarian sat smiling, ready to help them.

"Good afternoon, Samuel. How is your ghost story coming along?"

"Finished," Sam answered with a shrug, but there was a ring of pride in his voice.

"Good," she said, sounding really pleased. "May I help you find something else today? We have a fine new shelf of adventure stories." She smiled encouragingly at Sam and then at Dick and Jackie, who shuffled awkwardly in the background.

"Where can I look up someone's address, please?" Sam asked politely. "Someone not in the phone book?"

"The City Directory?" The librarian looked puzzled.

"Yes, ma'am," said Sam. "Guess that's it. Is there one here, please?"

"There is. Why certainly there is. But what on earth—" She broke off, staring curiously at Sam, who stared calmly back from behind his glasses, volunteering no information. "It's in the Reference Room. 096. But you can't take it out, you know."

"Yes, ma'am. Thank you." Sam trudged off toward the room marked "Reference."

As they hurried after Sam, Jackie had an idea. She wouldn't tell Dick. He might make fun of her. But the first rainy day she decided to come back and investigate that Adventure Shelf.

In the room marked "Reference," Sam walked slowly along rows of big fat dictionaries, muttering letters to himself.

"Here, at last!" His voice penetrated strangely through the book-lined room. He pulled out a huge volume and carried it to a table. Shoving up a chair, he sat down as if the place belonged to him.

"Walthers, Washburn, *Washington*," Sammy muttered as he thumbed through the pages with square, experienced fingers. "Gosh, there're quite a few Washingtons. Andrew, Daniel, Frederick, Helen, Mrs.—"

Suddenly he looked up, his round face breaking into smiles. "Gosh," he exclaimed, "there isn't any Go or any other first names, beginning with a 'G.'" He looked excitedly at Jackie, his dark eyes flashing.

After getting them all the way to the library to find the Washington they wanted to question, Sam seemed strangely glad there was no such man to find. Jackie stared at him curiously.

She knew that searching for mysteries inside the quiet walls of the library was more to Sam's liking than searching for them within a deserted, haunted house.

But still, he had set out to find this Washington, to learn if his name really was forged.

Why should Sam be so glad there was no such living man? Unless perhaps he wanted him to turn out to be someone who was no longer alive. Unless perhaps he thought—Jackie gasped and caught hold of Sam's shoulder.

"You mean," she whispered tensely, "that it was the real George Washington, first President of the United States?"

"Might have been," Sam admitted, trying not to let his voice reflect the excitement in his eyes.

"Why go worrying about a dead man?" With a shrug Dick turned to go.

"We're the *Ghostly* Trio," Sam reminded him significantly. "If the forger copied all these names from letters he found in the Kings' house," Sam's eyes sought Jackie's, "and if the house really was as old as you say, he *might* have copied the name from an old letter of the real Washington without knowing it was any different than letters from Mr. Blake or Dr. Miland."

"You're goofy." Dick tapped his head meaningfully. "A real President wouldn't have written a letter to anyone around here."

"He might have." But a shadow of doubt crossed Sam's face, erasing his wide, excited grin.

"Dr. Miland might know," Jackie suggested. "Anyway, he loves to talk about history and the King place."

"Then what are we waiting for?" Dick started for the door, taking a daring slide on the marble floor. Jackie followed along behind, almost reluctant to leave. There certainly were possibilities in the library she had never thought about before.

"Did you find what you wanted?" the librarian called cheerfully as they trooped past her desk.

"Yes, ma'am. Thank you." Sam answered politely, his face a blank. Only his eyes, hidden behind the reflection in his glasses, spoke of how much he had found.

10. YOUNG HISTORIANS

I T WAS LATE Saturday afternoon and the village
was crowded with week-end shoppers. The Trio
walked their bikes across the square to the drugstore on the other side. Jackie spun restlessly on a stool
at the soda fountain while Dr. Miland waited on four
or five people ahead of them. Sam had his notebook
out again and was making notes in quick, excited ab-
breviations.

"Say Doc, how old is the King place?" Sam asked as
Dr. Miland fished their popsicles out of the freezer.

"Plenty old." Dr. Miland smiled reminiscently.
"Course, some was added later, but that first wing, that
was there near two hundred years ago. Built by the first
Mr. King. Kingsville was named after—" He broke off,
his eye on a waiting customer.

"Dr. Miland," Sam prompted, "did George Washington know those Kings?"

"Well, now you mention it—" Dr. Miland paused to
take off his glasses and wipe his forehead. "Some claim
he spent a night there once, back in 1770 something, I
believe, on his way to Philadelphia. But we never could
be quite sure."

"Did he?" cried the Ghostly Trio, excitement high in

their voices. "Good-bye and thanks." They turned toward the door.

"Young historians, eh?" Dr. Miland muttered with an approving smile. "But now wait a minute." His voice unaccountably changed from the playful to the stern.

Reluctantly the Trio turned to face him.

"Say, what are you kids up to?" The druggist's scrubbed pink face was oddly grave. "Yesterday you came around asking about the Kings' old tenant house. Rufus Niel said there'd been two boys and a girl fooling around there this morning. Broke right into the place."

The Trio stared at the floor, unwilling to meet their friend's accusing gaze. Jackie sucked busily at her popsicle, but not with pleasure.

"You kids better not go fooling around where you don't belong," the druggist warned, his voice serious. "That Rufus Niel is a pretty tough customer. Old Mason was his friend and he's taking care of the place while the family's away."

"Why did they go away?"

"Where did they go in such a hurry?"

"Were the police after him?"

"I haven't time to gossip with you kids." Dr. Miland raised a plump hand as if to stop the flow of questions. "Anyway, stop asking things that don't concern you." He spoke sharply. "Remember what I said about Rufus. If he ever catches you, no telling what he might do," he added in a voice that gave no hint of whether he was serious or teasing.

Dumbly, the Trio nodded. Their faces shadowed with

guilt, they went thoughtfully through the revolving doors.

Pictures of the Mystery House and the horrible Rufus who guarded it spun in their heads as they walked their bicycles up the hill toward home. For a time nobody spoke.

"Somewhere," Sam said at last. He stood still to give his words more emphasis, and the others waited beside him. "Somewhere in that room where we found the other papers, there's a real treasure."

"Treasure?" questioned Dick, remembering the unyielding plaster walls of the dirty study.

"We know that forger had to copy 'Washington' from something." Sam spoke slowly. "We know there isn't any G. Washington around here."

The others nodded, frowning.

"And now we know that the real Washington *might* have written to those Kings," Sam continued.

Jackie, who was beginning to understand, stared at him, her eyes wide.

"Yes, sir." Sam moved on again. "It means that that caretaker guy might have had a real Washington letter, hundreds of years old, right in that old locked room. He might have stolen it with the other letters, never knowing what it was."

"What good's a letter?" Dick asked grumpily.

"But Dick," Jackie intervened. "A real Washington letter! Oh, boy, that *would* be a treasure, I guess."

They had reached the drive at the top of the hill, but Jackie went on home with the boys to Wildwood. She couldn't bear to end so soon the fascinating talk of their discovery. It was like something in a book.

"There's only one thing to do," Sam announced as the three settled themselves on the upper bunk for a conference. "We gotta go back and look for that letter—the real one the forger must have had."

"But Sam—" Dick looked at his brother with unbelieving eyes. "You were afraid of that house before—before we knew about Rufus guarding it."

"It's a historical mission," Sam answered gravely, but no one laughed at him. "If we can find that letter, it will be proof that George Washington really knew those Kings. Besides, that letter is a treasure, a real treasure, same as those kids found in that book I was telling you about. Only," he added huskily, "we'll have to go look for it at night, late, when that Rufus is asleep."

"But what about our families?" Jackie seized upon a convenient excuse.

"Ma and Pa are always asleep by ten," Dick said confidentially. "Adventure, brother! That's my line!" He slid from the bunk and began rooting in the bureau for his flashlight.

"But—" Jackie protested lamely. The flashlight, suddenly coming to view beneath a heap of underwear, was too real a reminder of the expedition before them. "My family go to bed much later than that." It gave her a nice safe feeling to know that her father was on watch till very late.

"Do you sleep with your sister?" Dick asked pointedly.

"N-no," Jackie faltered, almost wishing she did. "Not usually." Actually, she and Miriam never slept together now the way they used to, whispering and giggling and Miriam telling stories.

"It'll be easy then," Dick assured her. "Tonight, as soon as we get out, we'll come around and whistle under your window. No. Hoot. Like an owl. Three times. Then you can sneak down the back way and nobody will know, even if they're awake."

"But—" repeated Jackie. She turned to Sam, trying to understand his sudden bravery. Or was it bluff?

"Just don't think about it," Sam advised kindly. "Just think about *him*."

"I am thinking about him," Jackie retorted. "I'm thinking about Rufus."

"No, no. I mean George Washington." Sam pulled his notebook out of his pocket and, balancing it on his knee, began making notes again, letting the word "go" stand for George Washington, just in case the book fell into enemy hands. After a few minutes of writing he looked up at Jackie. She was staring unseeingly into space.

"How about it, Jackie?" he whispered. "Are you with us?"

There was a long silence while Jackie slowly brought her eyes back into focus. She turned them first on one brother, then on the other.

"Yes," she answered after agonizing seconds. "I'm with you!"

11. UNDER COVER OF NIGHT

JACKIE LAY shivering in bed. Shivering although the covers were drawn up all the way to her chin to hide her red plaid shirt. Shivering although she wore her dungarees and both pairs of red wool underwear her grandmother had given her for Christmas.

Jackie wasn't really cold. She was shivering with fear and excitement and, worst of all, with indecision. No matter how hard she tried to think ahead, she was still not sure what she would do when she heard the three owl hoots on the lawn below.

If she blinked her light on, it would be a signal to the boys that the family was watching, a signal that she couldn't leave. But if her room remained dark, it would mean she was making her way down the kitchen stairs to meet them in the evergreens beside the garage.

There was company downstairs tonight. Mother and Father were playing bridge. They called their cards solemnly between broken threads of grown-up conversation. Jackie sighed. She knew she was far from their thoughts. She turned her head uneasily toward the open window, listening for the signal.

There was a hushed stillness about the night, broken only by the long travel-hungry wail of a faraway engine and the echoing rattle of freight cars rumbling through the distant hills. And just outside the door came the soft padding sound of Miriam's slippered feet flopping purposefully down the hall.

Like Jackie, Miriam was supposed to be in bed. But she too was taking advantage of the bridge party. Jackie knew she was probably writing a poem, or a novel, things she thought she could do only late at night.

There was a rustling in the bushes beneath the window, and Jackie propped herself up on an elbow to listen just as the door opened and Miriam marched into the room as if it belonged to her. Jackie sank back into the pillow, pulling the sheet up like a collar around her neck to hide the red shirt.

Miriam switched on the light and went over to the desk while Jackie crept still farther under the covers. She wondered whether Sam and Dick would see the light and take it as a signal to go away. She didn't know whether she wished they would or wished they wouldn't. Closing her eyes, she muttered a little prayer to herself. A prayer that Miriam wouldn't notice her shoes and heavy sweater laid in readiness on a chair by the door. But Miriam, absorbed in her own thoughts, borrowed the ink out of the drawer and turned out the light again.

"Good night, Jackie darling, sweet dreams." With an odd toss of her very brushed yellow hair, Miriam spoke in a low theatrical whisper from the lighted hall.

Jackie, who decided Miriam probably was copying some movie star, didn't condescend to answer. She lay listening to Miriam's feet going back down the hall and the click of the door closing firmly behind her. Miriam too wanted to be alone. For a moment all was quiet except for the hum of an automobile speeding by on the Pike.

Then out of the stillness of the night the owl hoot penetrated the open window. Three times, clear and close and human. Miriam's turning on the light had not changed anything. Dick and Sam were waiting out there, expecting her to come.

"Oh, help me! Help me!" Jackie whispered to no one in particular. "Don't make me go."

Her groping hand found the light above her head and then the switch. She held it there for half a tantalizing second as if she were about to signal she couldn't come. But something strong inside her wouldn't let her press it. Mechanically Jackie climbed out of bed and picked up her shoes and sweater by the door. In stocking feet she tiptoed past Miriam's room, down the dark kitchen stairs and out the back door.

Jackie jumped in spite of herself as Dick and Sam emerged from the bushes. But even in the darkness their blurred shadows among the shrubbery were easy to recognize. Dick, slim and half a head taller, crept silently, swiftly toward her. Short and stocky, Sam stumbled clumsily behind, rustling the bushes and scuffing the ground as he came.

Without a word of greeting, they walked single file down the driveway and crossed the Pike. Skirting around the deserted back yards of Wildwood, they came once again to the meadow path that led across the swampy waste to Garden Manor and the pine-covered knoll.

Even in the daytime the meadow, too low and wet for houses and people, had a far-off jungly look. Now in the night, as the Trio left the last skeleton houses of Wildwood, it was black and ominous, full of darting, whispering shadows.

Dick paused on the path ahead and, as Jackie came up, silently handed her a flashlight. Reluctantly, the three moved forward, their lights throwing round pools of brightness on the ground, making the darkness beyond seem even blacker than before.

Jackie stepped ahead, then stopped to listen, then went on, only to stop and hesitate again. Although there was no wind, no sign of breeze, here and there a bush would rustle without reason or a twig would crack alarmingly. After what seemed a century of walking they somehow reached the edge of the meadow and started up the path toward the Mystery House. Playing their flashlights uneasily about them, they picked out familiar trees, landmarks of the trail.

Halfway up the slope Sam broke the brooding silence. "Better dim the lights in case that Rufus might be making his rounds."

Instantly the three flashlights blinked out. Below, through the trees, they could see lines of lights marking the new streets of Garden Manor.

"But Sam," Jackie's voice came out of the night, childish and plaintive, "you said Rufus would be in bed by now."

Without answering, Sam stumbled past the others into the heavy shadows ahead. As their eyes became accustomed to the dark again, Jackie noticed that the tangled hedge had taken the place of trees along the trail. Behind the hedge she knew the house lay still and waiting. Then Sam, who a second ago had been only three feet ahead of her, disappeared through the small gap they had come to know so well by daylight.

On a sudden impulse, Jackie grabbed at Dick to hold him back. Their mission now seemed far too dangerous to complete. But Dick already was hurrying after Sam as if ashamed to have him lead. Jackie followed on strange, unwieldy legs. There seemed nothing else for her to do.

With slow, groping steps they crossed the yard, black under its ceiling of pines. Afraid of the sound of their own footsteps on the rickety porch, Dick and Sam crawled on hands and knees around to their special window.

Jackie sensed rather than saw what they were doing. Mechanically she followed them. It was like a nightmare, horrible and frightening, but strange and quite unreal. It seemed to Jackie that her body, which was propelled against its will along the sagging porch to the window, belonged to someone else and not to her at all. It was as if she were a bystander, interested but remote.

Jackie could just make out the dark figures of Sam and Dick pushing on the window which someone had closed since their flight that morning. On their other visits, Sam's timidity had made Jackie feel brave. But now, as if by a miracle, he was up in front with Dick, helping to break into a terribly haunted house in the dead of night. Behind the pounding of Jackie's heart, behind her fear, there was a still less pleasant feeling. A feeling that she, Jacqueline Murray, was no longer part of the Ghostly Trio. A feeling that suddenly she was deserted and alone.

"Dick," she whispered moving up closer.

For answer there was a sharp squeak followed by a thin grinding groan as the window was slowly raised, revealing a greater blackness within.

"Dick! Sam!" All Jackie could see was the vague outline of two figures climbing over the sill and disappearing into the blackness on the other side. Jackie's fear of being alone pushed in at her from all sides. It was greater now than the fear of the house or any ghosts that might lie within. The next second, without quite knowing how she got there, Jackie was in the house beside the boys.

It was dark outside, but inside the darkness was complete. Jackie couldn't see where the boys were standing, although from their heavy breathing she could tell that they were close. Her outstretched hand, shaking and groping, clutched at Dick's jacket, her other hand found Sam's shoulder. The boys stood close together, invisible and very still, and Jackie had a peculiar feeling that the brothers were holding hands unseen there in the dark.

For long, long moments the Ghostly Trio stood motionless, listening and waiting. For what? They didn't know. In the dark the house didn't smell as musty as it had by day, and compared to the cold night air outside, it seemed unusually warm. Jackie had a feeling, impossible to explain, for the house was too dark for her to make out even the dim outline of the shabby furniture, that something had been changed. Had someone besides themselves learned of the treasure in that attic room? Had someone come to search the house before them? How long must they wait to learn the truth?

Jackie's thoughts swirled wildly through her head. But among them all, only one was clear. They couldn't stand like this indefinitely. They would have to go on or they would have to go back. Horrified by the minutes that were rushing by while they stood doing nothing, Jackie gave Dick a small brave shove.

It was then that they heard it. Perhaps it was what they had been waiting for. A noise so small, yet so cruelly real, their blood congealed within them. A noise that for all its smallness was a thousand times as frightening as the noise of the shutter banging or the squeak of the pump handle.

There was a step on the floor above them, a quiet, muffled step of a person who had removed his shoes. A step so soft, yet so clear, that even Jackie couldn't have imagined it.

Instinctively the Ghostly Trio tightened their grips on one another. Their eyes fixed in horror upon the darkness, their hearts jumped up into their throats so that even a whisper was impossible. Their legs turned lifeless and useless. They heard the noise again. But was it man or ghost? Slowly it was coming down the stairs. One muffled, padded foot at a time, with long horrible silences in between.

"Oh, let this be a nightmare," Jackie prayed with lips that moved but made no sound. "Oh, let me wake up safe in bed."

As if in a nightmare, the Ghostly Trio had forgotten how to run. Frozen to the spot, they waited through another long, long silence without a step, without a sound. It wasn't a noise but only a feeling that told Jackie someone was in the room with them. Someone was staring at them through the dark. But the others must have felt it too. Suddenly their minds reached down and told their feet to move, and all three, Dick in the lead, went tumbling toward the window and safety.

The window wasn't there. Not where Dick thought it had been. With Jackie and Sam pushing from behind, Dick worked his hands frantically along the wall in search of the evasive window sill. Some ghostly trick had cut off their escape.

"Who is it? Who is it?" came a wavering voice from the other side of the room. There was a scream from upstairs, a scream of fright, that made the goose-prickles rise still higher on the Trio's backs. Motionless they stood waiting for the inevitable.

There was a fumbling sound across the room. A clicking of matches shaken in a box. A long scratch and a spurt of flame. A moment later a kerosene lamp flicked, blinked dimly and flared up, sending long threatening shadows across the room.

12. DISCOVERED

A GHOST stood before them, light in hand. A woman's ghost, whose feet beneath her long white gown were bare and long and very thin. Her face too was long and thin. Her hair, long and dark, hung lifeless over her white shoulders.

The Trio stared, their mouths open. The ghost stared back, black eyes flashing wickedly in the flickering light. Her mouth was open, too, showing a round black chasm, but slowly it moved to form low ghostly words.

"Oh," it said, "it's children." With that the ghost sank into a convenient chair and unaccountably began to weep.

The Trio saw the window now, open and inviting, not three feet from where they stood. Shakily they moved toward it, glancing back over their shoulders at the figure in the chair. She had put the lamp down on the table and buried her face in her bony hands. It seemed an awful way to leave a person, even a ghost, and she certainly didn't seem very harmful now.

"Jeepers," said Jackie. Finding her voice, she directed it unsteadily toward the creature in the chair. "Is anything wrong?"

"Wrong?" answered the ghost, suddenly sitting erect. "You nearly frightened the life out of me."

"Oh," said Jackie, relieved. "Then you're not a ghost. I'm sorry. You frightened us too, you know."

The woman let herself smile, a thin smile over toothless gums, before her face turned angry.

"What are you doing here, you thieving little brats?" Standing up, she advanced toward them unsteadily with doubled fist. "If I had a phone, the police would be here in five minutes to put an end to your pranks."

Again there was a scream from above.

"It's all right, Edna. It's all right," the woman called over her shoulder and then turned again to face the Trio.

Dick backed hurriedly toward the window. But Jackie stood bravely facing their accuser. The thing had better be explained.

"Please," she whispered in a voice hardly loud enough to be heard. "We're not thieves. We're—we're —we're the Ghostly Trio," she finished helplessly.

"Yes," said Dick, with one leg securely over the window sill. "We were just looking for ghosts." The idea of ghosts had amused Mr. Blake. He thought perhaps it would help now.

The woman's face remained serious. "Who says there's ghosts here?" she asked sharply as if she were ready to believe there really were.

The Ghostly Trio stared at each other uneasily through the flickering light.

"Take your foot off that sill and kindly close the window and explain yourself," the woman said, speaking to Dick. "Do you want to freeze us all to death?"

Without knowing why, for there was nothing Dick wanted more than to disappear into the thick black woods outside, he obeyed.

"Now," the woman continued, pointing a lean finger at Dick, "who seen a ghost?"

"Nobody, nobody," Dick reassured her. "We just *wanted* to see one."

"Who are you, anyway?" Sam spoke for the first time, his dark eyebrows puckered, his glasses reflecting the light of the lamp.

"I'm Mrs. Mason, I am," the woman answered haughtily. "This is our house. You have no right. It was in the will. Old Mr. King left it to Dad."

"Oh," said Jackie. "We didn't know you still lived here. We're sorry to have frightened you."

"We're sorry. We're sorry," Dick muttered over and over again in his confusion.

"We'd better say good night." Jackie looked uncertainly toward the door now that the window was closed.

Mrs. Mason went over to the door and unbolted it for them. "You better not go fooling with any more windows," she told them sternly.

Still muttering incoherent apologies, Jackie and Dick edged toward the door, their eyes cast down to avoid the woman's angry stare. But Sam didn't move from where he stood. Eagerly he looked about the room as if in search of something that would keep him there. Suddenly Jackie remembered George Washington, whom she had quite forgotten in her fright. Sam's mind was a more tenacious one. The woman stared at him curiously, waiting for him to follow the others.

"We have caused you great inconvenience," Sam said at last. He spoke very slowly because he was not sure what he was going to say next.

Mrs. Mason continued to stare.

"We're sorry, very sorry," Sam went on unnecessarily, for Jackie and Dick had said it too often already. "We would like to be able to do something for you to make up for—to make up for the—the—the shock we've caused you."

"Is that so?" said the woman. Still she stared at Sam.

"Perhaps," Sam went on gropingly, "perhaps we could come back tomorrow and—and—" A tiny smile flitted across his broad face. "And do some chores for you," he concluded triumphantly.

"Oh, yes," Jackie added happily. "We'd like to help." Her voice was eager, almost pleading. Once more George Washington seemed very near.

"To make up for the harm we've done," Sam explained quickly.

"Well." The woman hesitated, staring first at one, then at another of her uninvited guests. "It is hard around here without a man. You don't really look like bad children."

"Oh, no," Jackie agreed eagerly. "We're not. Really we're not."

"How about tomorrow?" asked Dick, who wanted to have a part in the planning. "Sunday school's in the morning, but we'll come right after dinner."

Mrs. Mason nodded vaguely and held the door open as they filed out. Jackie had a funny feeling the woman was going to cry again. She scurried out of the house and across the dark yard as fast as she could go with Dick and Sam on either side.

A big halfmoon was rising over the meadow, and they jogged quickly home in half the time it had taken them to come. As they reached the half-finished buildings on the edge of Wildwood, Jackie looked hesitantly at her two companions. She was wondering if the boys would go home and leave her to find the rest of the way alone. But Dick and Sam walked staunchly by her side and didn't turn to go until she stood safely on her own back steps.

"See you tomorrow," Jackie whispered by way of good night.

"Right after dinner," Sam whispered back. "The longer we work, the more time we'll have to look for Go," he added wisely, and he and Dick ran off toward their waiting beds.

Jackie watched the two brothers fondly, as they trotted along side by side, until they disappeared among the shadows of the maples. Then, taking off her shoes, she turned to open the kitchen door.

It was locked.

Unalarmed, Jackie wiggled her feet back into her wet shoes and went around to the front door. She tried the long French windows that opened out onto the terrace, and the little sash window on the side porch. Every door was locked, every window firmly latched.

Again and again she walked around the house. She felt far too old and tired now to be afraid of the shadows that fell in tangled patterns upon the white clapboards, or of the hoot of a real owl in the tree above her head. Only when she passed under the open window of her parents' room did she hold her breath and tiptoe.

Around the corner Miriam's window too was open to the night air.

"Miriam," Jackie whispered to herself. Miriam was her only chance. "Miriam," she called aloud in a husky whisper. Then a little louder. "Miriam. Miriam!"

"What—what?" Miriam's voice floated down, baffled and heavy with sleep. "What is it? Where are you?"

"Here," said Jackie forgetting to whisper. "Here. Outside."

A moment later Miriam's head appeared at the window.

"Jackie!" she whispered. "What in heaven's name?"

"Shh—" Jackie pleaded. "Please don't tell. Just come down and let me in."

"But what are you doing out there in the middle of the night?" Miriam was quite awake now. Her voice was pitched high, full of curiosity.

"Never mind," Jackie answered. "Just let me in. Please. Quick."

There was a long silence while Miriam stared down calculatingly at Jackie, helpless on the lawn below.

"I'll tell you what." Miriam spoke at last, her voice low and confidential. "I'll let you in if—" she paused meaningfully. "If you'll tell me where you've been tonight and what you do with those boys every day at the library and drugstore and all. Janet's mother said she saw you there with them."

"So that's it," Jackie whispered to herself. All along when Mim had pretended not to notice, not to care what she did, she was wondering and watching and waiting for a chance like this. But Jackie knew one of Miriam's secrets too. How glad she was now that Mr. Blake had sent them to the shack in the field.

"I know where your clubhouse is," she challenged. "If you don't let me in, I'll tell all the kids in the neighborhood. It's in the field behind the briar patch."

Miriam gave a little snort of laughter. "See if I care. It's not a secret any more. Someone already knows. They've been banging around trying to scare us."

Then Jackie remembered the stones they had thrown and she felt far more foolish than Miriam could know. Her own pranks were playing against her. If it hadn't been for those stones she might have traded secrets now.

"Well," said Miriam when Jackie didn't speak. "Guess I'll get some sleep." She put her hands on the window as if to close it.

Shivering, Jackie watched as Miriam lowered the window inch by inch.

"All right, you beast," Jackie agreed despairingly just before the window closed. "I'll tell you if you cross your heart and hope to die if you tell anyone, even your darling social club."

"Not even them," Miriam answered in a stage whisper. "I'll come down the back way."

Jackie hurried around to the kitchen steps and waited by the door. At last she could hear Miriam's bare feet crossing the kitchen, then the jiggling of the lock. The bolt slipped back and Jackie was inside. She never had thought that any house could feel quite so good and safe and warm. Together the two girls tiptoed up the back stairs, down which Jackie had escaped less than two hours before.

Miriam followed Jackie into her room, closing the door carefully behind her. She turned on the night light and stood watching silently as Jackie pulled off her heavy outdoor clothes. Jackie eyed her older sister curiously, wondering why she didn't go, and crept shivering into bed.

Still without words, Miriam turned off the light and climbed in beside her. She lay very still in the darkness, one arm around Jackie, waiting for her to begin. It was just the way it used to be when they were younger. Only this time Jackie was the storyteller. And this time the story had no ending. That was still to come.

13. THE MASONS

BEFORE she even opened her eyes, Jackie had a feeling it was late. Yawning, she slowly lifted her heavy lids and looked about. The window was closed, the room already warm. Miriam stood by the mirror, dressing in her Sunday clothes. This was odd because Miriam always dressed privately in her own room across the hall.

"After Sunday school I'll wear my blue jeans and red shirt," Miriam was saying as if she had been talking for some time. "They look nice, and still it won't hurt if I have to do any dirty work."

Then Jackie remembered. They were going back to the Mystery House. They were going to help the ghost-like Mrs. Mason while secretly they searched for the precious letter Sam felt so sure was there.

Squinting into the sunlight, Jackie watched Miriam uneasily. She was busy brushing out the kinks the curlers had made, into soft loose waves. Apparently, quite uninvited, Miriam was coming too. What would Dick and Sam say to that?

But Jackie had no chance to slip away to warn them. Right after breakfast there was Sunday school. Then there was helping Mother in the kitchen and the big noon dinner to get through. When Jackie finally started off toward Wildwood, Miriam came skipping out to join her.

"You coming too?" Jackie asked, not knowing whether to be glad or sad.

Miriam nodded, smiling rather foolishly.

"You going to help us hunt?"

"Well—" Miriam hesitated. "I don't believe in that letter your friend seems so sure about. But I'd like to see that house and that ghost woman and all."

"You'll help us hunt?" Jackie insisted.

"All right," Miriam gave in. "I'll help for all the good it will do. But this Go Washington business is silly."

The sun was bright, the air springlike and so warm they took off their sweaters as Jackie led the way across the Pike. Stamping down the new cement sidewalk of Wildwood Jackie sang lustily:

> "Fifteen men on a dead man's chest
> Yo, ho, ho and a bottle of rum."

She glanced at Miriam, hoping she would join in the way she used to do. Miriam smiled back. But she didn't join in. Perhaps she had forgotten how.

As they reached Number Twenty-eight, Dick and Sam came rushing out, evidences of chocolate ice cream on their lips. At sight of Miriam they stopped.

"Mim, this is Dick. This is Sam." Jackie felt stiff and silly introducing them as they stood grimly looking each other over. In the awkward silence that followed, Miriam pulled her dime-store compact from her blue jeans and began busily powdering her nose.

Jackie fumed inwardly. She had wanted them to like her sister. "She discovered about last night so I had to let her come," she said to the boys. "Come on," she added, loud and cheerful. "Let's get going."

Once they had started along the meadow trail everything seemed right again. For Miriam's benefit (and for their own pleasure too) the boys retold the story of their adventure in the Mystery House and the clues that had led up to it. And Miriam was so impressed she forgot about acting grown up and the compact that jiggled in her pocket. Maybe she too was beginning to believe in the letter and G. Washington.

The story barely finished, they reached the tangled, overgrown hedge with the drab little house behind it. But after the lurid pictures they had painted for Miriam, after the wonderful memories of haunts and fears, it was sadly disappointing.

The Mystery House didn't look very mysterious today, or very haunted either. Nor did it look like a house that concealed a hidden treasure. The shutters were fastened back and all the windows opened wide to the early spring sunshine. The yard, once so bleak and bare, was crisscrossed with clotheslines strung up between the pine trees. From them dangled shirts and towels and underwear. All most unmysterious!

There was a sound of young voices in the woods behind the house, and from an open window came the vigorous swishing of a broom.

"Well." Sam looked uncertainly at Jackie. "Here we are. Guess we knock, this time."

"Yes," agreed Jackie. "No more climbing in the windows now." She marched across the yard and up the rickety steps, and knocked boldly at the door. The noise of sweeping stopped.

"Who could that be?" They heard a girl's voice, high and anxious, as if a knock was something to be feared. Then the familiar voice of the woman. "Guess I'll have to see."

A minute later the door opened and the ghost of last night stood before them. But she didn't look so ghostly today in her ragged black sweater, and patched and faded skirt. Her long hair was pinned up into a tight knot at the back of her head. When she spoke, Jackie noticed with surprise that she was no longer toothless.

"Oh, so you did come back." The woman sounded astonished. "I never thought you would. But I don't remember that one," she added, turning suspicious eyes on Mim.

"This is my sister, Miriam Murray," Jackie explained. "She's—she's playing with us today."

"How do you do," said Miriam with a little bob of a curtsy. It looked silly. Especially in jeans.

"Murray, eh?" Mrs. Mason looked hard at Mim the way grownups so often did. "Well, at least you don't go tearing around in the middle of the night scaring people half to death."

A young girl about Jackie's age tiptoed up behind Mrs. Mason. She stood looking timidly at them from behind her mother.

"This is Edna, my oldest."

"Hello," said Jackie leaning over to one side to get a better look at her.

Edna regarded them distrustfully. Her brown hair fell softly about her pale thin face and over her narrow shoulders. She smiled uncertainly at them. Jackie noticed with a little shock how crooked her teeth were.

"You entertain our guests." Mrs. Mason gave Edna a little shove toward the others. "I'll start in with the scrubbing."

"We're not guests. We—we've come to—" Sam's words of protest tumbled all over each other, but Mrs. Mason had already disappeared into the house.

Edna stood first on one foot, then on the other, eyeing the four guardedly. Her legs looked very long and spindly under her too-short plaid skirt. Half of one foot protruded from the side of a battered shoe. She must have noticed Jackie looking at it because she herself glanced down at her feet.

"These aren't my best shoes," she announced defensively.

The Ghostly Trio stared uncomfortably, not knowing

what to say. It was Miriam who came to their rescue.

"Why, of course they're not." She smiled at Edna, her sweetest, most beautiful grown-up smile.

Edna was not reassured. "Just what did you all come for?" Her voice was suspicious.

"We came to help you," Miriam answered, sounding as if she were playing a part in a play. "You will let us help you, won't you?" Her voice struck a theatrical note.

Jackie squirmed and glanced sideways at the boys. This wasn't the way they had thought things would be.

"We don't need help," Edna announced with unexpected boldness and turned quickly toward the house.

"Hey, come back." In panic lest they lose Edna, and with her the treasure they had come to find, Jackie sprang forward, grabbing the girl by a skinny arm.

Edna was forced to look at her. Her deep-set brown eyes staring out of her white face were so bewildered and resentful that Jackie had to laugh. Edna studied Jackie's merry face, and a faint smile flickered on her own thin lips.

"We've just come to pay our debt." Jackie spoke quickly, taking advantage of that fleeting smile.

"Debt?" The girl's voice was so low the others could scarcely hear it.

"Yes," Sam answered. "We were er—er—er—playing a kind of game last night and frightened your mother nearly to death."

"Not meaning to, of course," Jackie added, smiling hard at Edna in the hope that she would smile back again.

"Yes," murmured Edna, her eyes on the ground, avoiding Jackie's. "You broke into our house, I know. But Ma said you wouldn't ever come back again, even though you said you would."

"Well, we did," Jackie exclaimed proudly. "Now what can we do?"

"Well." Edna pulled her arm away from Jackie. "There's plenty wants doing. Let me see." She sat down on the rickety porch steps and rested her little pointed chin on her bony knees.

Encouraged, the Ghostly Trio sat down beside her, and so did Miriam, gingerly. Edna looked at each of them as if studying what each might do best.

"Those two boys," she pointed first to Sam and then to Dick, "had better help the twins out back."

"Twins!" cried Dick with rising interest.

Sam scowled. He didn't want to work "out back." He wanted to work inside. In one room in particular, second floor right. He glanced at his brother reprovingly. Already Dick seemed to have forgotten the whole point of their visit.

"Yeah, Timmy and Tommy," Edna explained to Dick, her voice slowly gaining confidence. "They're trying to build up a woodpile and Timmy has an ax. But he won't let you use it."

Pulling a small tin whistle from her pocket, she blew on it vigorously.

There were answering hoots from the woods and a few minutes later two ragged boys came around the corner of the house. They were arguing over the possession of a small hatchet which they both tugged at determinedly. Both had thick rumpled dark hair that needed cutting, twinkling black mischievous eyes and round, dirt-smeared faces. Both were the same height, about half a head shorter than Jackie herself.

"Goodness," Jackie gave a delighted gasp. "They are twins. Which is which?"

"I'm Tim," said one. He screwed up his eyes and giggled so Jackie knew he was Tom.

"I'm Tom," said Tim.

It was evidently a family joke.

"These boys are going to help you," Edna announced, smiling at them indulgently.

Dick jumped to his feet, eager for action. Brandishing the ax and yelling like Indians, the twins led the way back into the woods.

"Well," Edna turned toward Sam, "aren't you going too? You said you wanted to help!"

"Sure," sighed Sam. "Sure I am." He adjusted his glasses and trudged reluctantly after Dick, but not before he had given Jackie a long pleading look.

Jackie knew what he meant. The letter must be found, and now it was up to her to find it. With an effort she turned toward Edna.

"Well," she asked brightly, "what can we do?"

Edna looked at Jackie and then at Mim. "The twins' trousers want patching," she answered after due consideration. "They're supposed to start back to school next week, but they can't until they get new knees in them. Tim needs a whole new seat in his blue pair."

"Is—is the sewing room upstairs?" Jackie had made up her mind she could do most anything if only she could get into that attic room.

"Silly," Edna giggled. "The light's best right out here on the steps. That is, if you can sew," she added suspiciously.

"I embroidered a beautiful hanky for Mother, Christmas," Miriam confessed.

"Those pants don't need embroidery." Edna gave a disgusted sniff. "Just plain patches. I already got them cut out of the legs of Grandpop's old trousers. The twins can't go to school 'til they get fixed. Ma said the truant officer probably will be coming around next week."

"Really!" Jackie's face lit with interest. "I read about one in the funnies but I never saw one."

"He's going to come after me too," Edna boasted, seeing the admiration in Jackie's eyes. "Ma says she won't let me take one step in that school with these.' She glanced down at her tattered shoe again. This time with pride.

"Oh, boy." Jackie stared admiringly at her. "Will he have a gun?"

"Yes," Edna answered matter-of-factly. "I think he's going to shoot me through the heart. I'll get the sewing. It's nice in the sun, not a bit like February."

"It's no use," Jackie called after her. "We can't fix those pants."

"Now what's the matter?" Edna paused in the doorway, a hand on each hip. "Thought you wanted to help."

"We do, honest we do," Jackie protested, her face almost as red as her hair. "It's just no use. I can't sew patches and neither can Mim."

"Go on! You're kidding!"

"But we can do hard work," Jackie offered with enthusiasm. "We can sweep and wash windows and scrub floors."

"Or make beds," added Miriam, who didn't feel like getting dirty.

"Ma's doing all that."

"I know." Jackie was not to be discouraged. "You tell your mother to come out and sit in the sun and sew. We'll do the cleaning. We'd like to, honest."

"I'll see what she says," Edna answered doubtfully. She went into the house, leaving Jackie and Mim alone on the steps.

"My goodness," whispered Mim. "She ought to have her teeth straightened."

"Listen." Jackie was urgent. "We've got to get upstairs. It's the room to the right. You can tell by the desk. We can go through the papers as we tidy up. Shh—"

The door opened and Edna came out again, her arms full of old clothes. Mrs. Mason followed.

"Now sit right down, Ma." Edna handed her the mending. "Give yourself a rest."

It never had occurred to Jackie to tell her own mother to give herself a rest. She made a resolution to try it sometime. But it was immediately forgotten as she followed Edna through the kitchen and up the dark familiar stairs.

14.   CASE CLOSED

A T THE TOP of the stairs Edna led the way into the bedroom on the left. The door to the other room, the important one, was closed so tightly that only a little crack of light showed on the floor beneath it. It was too dark to see if they had bolted it again.

The four iron cots were neatly made and covered with patched and faded spreads. By the door a bucket, a box of soap powder, a pile of rags, a mop and a mysterious bottle marked "poison" stood in readiness.

"Guess Ma's done all but the scrubbing." Edna looked around the room with a professional eye. "I'll take the mop, and you," she pointed to Jackie, "take some of those rags and dry up after me. And you—" She stared at Mim appraisingly. "Guess you might as well start on the windows." She poured some water from the bucket and some of the stuff out of the bottle marked "poison" into a basin and handed it to Miriam.

Jackie, who knew that Miriam had never washed a window, stared at her with sympathy.

"Come on, Jackie." Edna tossed a rag in her direction. "You *are* Jackie, aren't you?"

Jackie nodded. The timid girl, who half an hour before had been hiding behind her mother, was suddenly far from timid.

"An empty house can sure get dirty in a year." Edna sighed as she rolled up her sleeves.

"Where were you all that time?" Jackie asked, her voice carefully casual.

"Visiting, out of state," Edna answered briefly and dunked her mop into the sudsy water.

"But why did you go so suddenly?" Jackie persisted.

"Grandpa was in a hurry," Edna answered without elaborating. "Then Ma got scared, so we went too."

"But why did you stay away so long?"

"I told you. Ma's scared living here in the woods without a man." Edna looked at Jackie accusingly. "That's why she was so frightened when you—"

"But," Jackie interrupted flushing at the reminder of last night's escapade, "then why did you come back now?"

"Had to get things ready for Grandpa." Edna swirled the soapy water with the mop.

"Oh, is he coming home?" Somehow Jackie managed to swallow a squeal of excitement.

"Sure. What'd you think?" Edna pulled the mop from the bucket and began swishing sudsy water about the floor.

"But where was he?" Jackie insisted, although somehow she felt she shouldn't ask.

"Come on," Edna spoke sharply. "Get to work if that's really why you came."

Jackie bit her lip, cross that she had let Edna see how

curious she was. She set to work with a will and for the next half hour, unmindful of the soggy wetness of her dungarees, dutifully followed Edna's mop about the room. On hands and knees Jackie crawled under the beds and into the corners, trying valiantly to blot up the puddles Edna splashed so easily upon the floor. But Jackie's mind was on the room across the hall.

Sticking her mop back into the bucket for the last time, Edna turned toward Miriam. Mim was still gingerly attacking the window, holding her reeking ammonia-soaked rag at arm's length from her face.

"Aren't you finished yet?" Edna's tone implied that she should be.

"I—I don't know." Miriam looked distressed. "I wish you'd see my fingers. They've all turned white and wrinkly."

In alarm, Jackie rushed to Miriam and saw that it was true. Her dainty fingers were white and puckered, and the natural pink polish had quite chipped off her tapering nails.

"That's the ammonia that does it," Edna explained carelessly. "Better go down and rinse them off," she advised, gathering up the dirty rags and tossing them into the still dirtier water in the bucket. "And better rub some lard on them. It's on the shelf over the pump."

"Pump?" Miriam sounded as if she'd never heard of one.

"Does it work?" Jackie asked, remembering how Sam and Dick had struggled with it.

"Of course it works," Edna answered scornfully.

"How do you think we got this scrubbing water? You can work it, can't you?"

"I don't know," Mim answered, staring tragically at her hands. "I never have."

"Brother, you girls don't know anything!" Edna remarked with satisfaction. "Come on down and I'll pump for you. Come on, Jackie."

"My hands are okay." Jackie reached for her last chance. "I'll stay here and pick up the rest of these rags."

"Okay, but make it snappy." Followed by Mim, Edna started down the stairs.

Jackie followed them out into the hall. Below in the kitchen she could hear the familiar squeak of the pump handle and then the rush of water and Miriam's scream as the cold water hit her hands.

For the second time in her life Jackie approached the forbidden door. Only this time she was quite alone. Neither Dick nor Sam was there to give her courage. Her heart began to beat the way it had the night before. Softly she put her hand on the latch.

The door, no longer bolted, swung open, and Jackie stared into a room that looked surprisingly bright and very, very clean. There was no littered desk, no boxes filled with papers. Again Jackie stopped to listen, but the sound of running water below told her that Edna was still busy at the pump. Slowly she went into the room, walking on tiptoe not to dirty the bare scrubbed floor. The desk she sought stood wedged into a corner, covered with a crisp white cloth. Uneasily Jackie raised the edge and pulled out a drawer. She tried a second

and then a third. Except for fresh newspaper on the bottom they were all bare, as bare as Mother Hubbard's famous cupboard. Gone were the papers, gone were the pens, gone were the dried-up inks of different colors. Gone for sure was the letter from George Washington, if there had ever been one.

The girls were calling to Jackie now, and Edna's voice sounded accusing to her guilty ears. Through the window she could hear the shouts of the boys drawing closer from the woods. Jackie tiptoed out of the room and hurried down the stairs to join the others.

In the kitchen Edna was supervising while Miriam dried her hands on a long roller towel. Sam and Dick and the twins stomped into the room, followed by Mrs. Mason. Her arms were piled high with the mending and the clean clothes from the line. Edna took half her load and together mother and daughter went upstairs.

"What happened?" whispered Sam moving close to Jackie.

"It's all cleaned out. Not a scrap left," Jackie answered. "Edna might know where the papers are, but she's as suspicious as—"

"Maybe the twins," Sam interrupted. "They're too young to understand."

For a moment Jackie studied the twins' happy, dirty faces.

"Where do you put your trash around here?" she asked, coming quickly to the point before Edna or Mrs. Mason came down again.

"You mean all those old papers in Grandpa's room?" Tim asked innocently.

The Ghostly Trio nodded.

"Ma burned them in the stove," Tom answered for his brother. "Say, what you guys want anyway?"

"Nothing." Sam's voice was flat and expressionless. "We gotta go now."

"We gotta go," repeated Jackie.

As they turned toward the door, Mrs. Mason came downstairs again, followed by a proud and smiling Edna.

"You're smart girls," she said, her gaunt face broader for its grin. "That room's clean as a whistle. And all that big pile of wood." She turned toward the boys. "I saw it from the window. With the time you saved me I'll be able to bake a cake. We'll have a housewarming. To-morrow afternoon."

"And I'll make the frosting," Edna volunteered. "A Washington's Birthday frosting, cause it's his birthday."

"Thank you, we'd love to," Miriam accepted prettily. Dick licked his lips in anticipation. But Jackie and Sam didn't answer. In fact, they had hardly heard the invitation above their own dark, gloomy thoughts.

"Just think," Sam murmured as they trudged home across the thawing, squashy meadow, "I had all the clues and now it's gone up in flames." His voice was husky, close to tears.

"But we still haven't cleared up all the mystery," Jackie said, trying to cheer him.

"Mystery?" Sam stared at her hopelessly. "The letter's gone, you dope. Burned. Everything's over." His voice wavered and he turned his face away.

Jackie slowed down to Sammy's gait and laid a consoling arm across his shoulder. "There's still some mystery left. We haven't proved why they left so suddenly."

"I told you." Rudely Sam brushed Jackie's arm from his shoulder. "If he was a forger and the police were after him, maybe the FBI too, he had to go. He was running away."

"But why do the grownups act so hush-hush about it?" demanded Dick.

"And where did they go?" insisted Jackie. "And where's old Mason been? Edna said he was coming home."

"Aw, go ask 'em," Sam answered dully.

"I did," said Jackie. "But Edna's awful funny. You can tell they don't want people prying into things."

"Well, I guess you wouldn't either," Miriam spoke up suddenly. "Not if your grandfather was a *criminal*." She shuddered.

"Criminal, pooh." Jackie bristled. "Anyway, it might be kind of exciting. Nothing exciting ever happens to us. In a way I envy them, sort of."

"I don't." Miriam liked feeling sorry for people. "They don't have any shoes, not decent ones, poor things, and I have two pairs I hardly ever wear. Tomorrow I'll take them to Edna and some of my old dresses too. That'll be fun."

"I've got some pants that are too short," said Dick. "But I think Ma's saving them for Sam."

"We ought to make a list," Miriam suggested gaily. "A list of all the things we can take to the Masons tomorrow. Anyone got a pencil?"

For a moment Sam stared at Mim, his round face a gloomy blank. Then slowly he reached into his pocket and pulled out the worn notebook and much-chewed stub of pencil. Sadly he thumbed through the pages. Notes about the Mystery House, the banging shutter, the forger's room. Clues, all of them, leading up to one great name, George Washington. And tomorrow was his birthday and everything was over.

Sam came to the end of his notes. He licked his pencil thoughtfully. Balancing the notebook on his knee, he wrote the words: "Case Closed."

"All right." He turned to Mim with a feeble effort at a smile. "We can proceed from here."

15. A SCRAP FOR SCRAP

THE NEXT AFTERNOON was damp and gloomy, but a happy procession of four made their way slowly across the meadow. Behind them they pulled Jackie's old express wagon heavily loaded with two bulging boxes. Miriam's and Jackie's contained sweaters and skirts, several pairs of shoes, Miriam's red wool dress and Jackie's two pairs of boxing gloves. It had been hard to give up the gloves, but now that Miriam was too grown up to box, Jackie knew there was little point in keeping them. There were clothes for the twins in the boys' box and a special big bag of marbles and a spinning top and a ball.

Feeling like four awkward Santa Clauses, they labored up the pine-covered slope toward the Mystery House that had lost its treasure in the kitchen stove.

By the time they reached the house a misty drizzle was coming down noiselessly. The small dark windows were closed today, the yard bare. The old deserted look was back again. Together the four of them hoisted the heavy wagon up onto the porch and stood uncertainly in front of the door.

Jackie raised a hand as if to knock, but her eye fell guiltily on the gifts in the wagon. How could they ever explain them to the Masons? She looked questioningly at the boys, who shuffled uneasily beside her, and then at Miriam. She alone seemed at ease.

"What's the matter with you all?" Miriam tapped with confidence on the door. "We aren't trying to steal anything. We're *giving* now."

"That's just it," Jackie admitted. "I don't know how to act."

"Let's just leave them out here until later," Sam suggested.

"But I do want to see Edna in my red wool dress," Mim protested, whispering now, for inside the house footsteps were moving toward the door. "If only her teeth were straighter, she wouldn't look half bad."

"She's fine the way she is," Jackie answered staunchly.

The latch jiggled and the door was opened. "I got the cake all baked before I went shopping," Mrs. Mason announced as she let them in. "Edna stayed home to make the frosting. Couldn't take her anyway. Not to Kingsville without a decent dress and everybody staring the way they did."

"Oh, but my red dress—"

But Miriam was interrupted by Edna, who came dancing barefooted into the room. She looked very clean and scrubbed and happy and somehow different. Her pale face had a pinkish tinge. Her hair, braided into two neat pigtails, was tied with bright red ribbons. Her faded summer dress was clean and freshly ironed. Beneath it her bare white legs seemed to twinkle with an airy gaiety.

"Just wait 'til you see it, wait 'til you see it," she singsonged, dancing about. "But you can't see it, you can't see it," she contradicted gleefully. "Not now. Not 'til teatime. I've got to finish brushing out Grandpop's clothes. He's coming home tomorrow and we've a real closet to surprise him. Rufus Niel brought it over last night."

At the mention of the familiar name, Jackie looked uneasily toward the boys, but they were too busy looking for the twins to notice.

"Where are they?" asked Dick.

"Out in the rain, piling some of that wood into the shed before it gets too wet," Mrs. Mason answered.

"Come on." Dick tugged at Sam's elbow. "Let's find 'em."

Jackie watched the boys regretfully as they ran across the yard. She would have liked to go with them, but somehow it didn't seem polite to leave Edna. Especially since she had made the frosting for the cake.

"Come on," said Edna grandly. "You can watch while I finish my work. Then we'll have the party."

As the two Murrays followed Edna through the kitchen, Jackie noticed that it was unusually hot, the windows misted with steam.

"Just had my bath," Edna announced.

"What?" Miriam's voice rose to a squeal. "In the kitchen?"

"Sure." Edna gave her one of those "you-don't-know-nothing" looks. "The stove was hot from the baking so it wasn't much trouble to heat the water."

"Of course," said Miriam wisely, as if she were used to heating water for her bath.

"It takes a lot though, to fill that big tub." With pride Edna pointed to a galvanized washtub under the stove.

"It—it's lovely." Miriam didn't sound convinced, but she had suddenly remembered her manners.

Jackie's face lit with pleasure. "Jeepers. You wouldn't let me try it sometime, would you?"

"Well." Edna hid her pleasure behind a doubtful frown. "It's a lot of work heating all that water."

"Oh, Jackie," Miriam shifted to her grown-up voice. "What will you ask next!"

"I'd like to come at night sometime too," Jackie went on, ignoring Mim, "and watch you light those lamps."

"Willigers!" Edna opened the door at the foot of the stairs. "You're daffy." But as they started up, she put an arm around Jackie's waist. The first real sign of friendship. "You can come as—as often as you like. We aren't going to move away again. Not ever. The trip on the bus was fun, especially coming home. But I hated living with Aunt Emmie and so did the twins."

"Aunt Emmie?" Jackie managed to keep her voice low to hide her interest.

"Yes, that's where we stayed when Grandpop was in—" Edna's mouth clamped shut. Her arm dropped from Jackie's waist, and she went scooting ahead of Jackie and Miriam up the stairs.

They hurried after her. Jackie sighed as she climbed the dark stairs, sad that she had acted so curious again just when Edna was being friends. But two of the puzzles were solved. Old Mason had been in prison. Sam was right. Even though the family had all run away in the middle of dinner, Mason had been found and arrested. Edna and the others had gone to live with a horrible aunt named Emmie. It was simple, but it still didn't explain why the grownups wouldn't talk about it.

Outside, Jackie could hear shouts as Dick and Sam greeted the twins. She wanted to tell them what they had learned. Now that the precious paper had been burned, even the old locked room where Edna took them had little fascination. A pile of shabby men's clothes was heaped on the cot. Wedged into a corner was an ugly corrugated paper closet.

"As soon as I get these brushed out and put away, we can have our party," Edna announced importantly.

"Will it take long?" Miriam asked leafing through a book of detective stories that lay on the desk.

"Not very," Edna answered. "You can sit on the bed if you don't put your feet up."

"Can't we help?" Already Jackie wiggled with impatience.

"No, thank you," Edna said smugly. "It's got to be done by someone that knows."

Miriam settled down on the bed with the book. Jackie sat restlessly beside her and watched Edna with admiration as she placed a coat on a hanger and deftly brushed it with a small whisk broom. One by one she turned the worn pockets inside out over a big sheet of newspaper. They were full of old paper clips, matchboxes and tobacco crumbs that fell onto the paper like winter sleet on a roof.

As Jackie watched, a crumpled paper, much like the

ones she had seen on the old desk, was whisked out of a pocket. Along with the tobacco crumbs it dropped to the floor.

Jackie didn't think. Mechanically she slid off the bed. Mechanically her hand closed over the yellowed scrap and slipped it into her blouse. Her eyes avoiding Edna, she eased herself back onto the bed, pretending nothing had happened. It was several seconds before she dared look up to see if Edna had noticed.

"What's the big idea?" Edna's deep eyes flashed. "That was Grandpop's."

"Silly." Jackie tried to laugh but she was too uneasy to make it sound convincing. "It was nothing but a scrap. You were going to throw it away, anyhow."

"I know," Edna admitted. "But why should *you* want it?"

"I—I don't," lied Jackie. "Not much. We just collect scrap. It's a habit of mine, isn't it?" she turned to Miriam for support, but Miriam, her head bent over the book, was oblivious to the argument.

"Well," Edna tossed her pigtails. "That's mighty funny. But I'm collecting scrap myself." She took a menacing step toward Jackie.

"Water's boiling. Time for tea." Mrs. Mason called up to them from the kitchen. "Better hurry."

"Come on." Edna's eyes had a dangerous glint. "Hand it over."

"Look." Jackie took a long breath. "I'll give you a sucker for it. An all-day sucker. I get my allowance tomorrow."

"Give me two." Edna stared at her, calculating.

"Two." Jackie nodded uneasily. "Tomorrow after school."

"No." Edna continued to stare. "A dozen. That's my final offer. A dozen suckers or I'll get that paper if I have to undress you."

Under her blouse Jackie could feel the disputed paper scratching tantalizingly against her bare skin. If she only could spread it out and look, she would know whether it was worth a dozen lollipops and many more, or whether it was as worthless as the old newspaper on the floor. It was a gamble she had to take.

"Okay," Jackie agreed with a sigh. "Twelve, but not one suck more."

"One dozen." Edna nodded with satisfaction. "After school tomorrow. Let's shake on it."

Jackie held out her hand and took Edna's in hers. It was strong and hard, and the skin felt rough and chapped and pulled tight over the bones.

"Haven't had a sucker in almost a year." Edna smiled, showing her crooked teeth.

"Well," answered Jackie, happy in spite of the bad bargain, "you wouldn't be getting them tomorrow if I wasn't an awful sucker myself."

Edna giggled. "You just don't know any better," she replied fondly. Going over to the bed, she gave Miriam a familiar nudge. "Haven't you ever seen a book before? Come on. We're going to eat."

Miriam closed the book reluctantly and followed the other two out of the room. In the gloom of the dark hall

Jackie lingered behind. She reached for the paper to have a look.

"Hey, come on down," Edna called back. "Why aren't you coming?"

"I am," Jackie answered, tucking the paper deeper into her blouse. There, she decided, it would have to stay until she was far from Edna's shrewd, observing eyes.

As Jackie came into the kitchen, she scarcely recognized the old wooden table now elegant under a snowy white cloth. There were bright paper flowers in the center and gaily painted china at every place.

"Oh," Jackie exclaimed, "how lovely it—" She broke off. The twins were sparring in the doorway. They wore her boxing gloves. "Jeepers." She turned toward Dick, half relieved, half disappointed. "You've given them the presents already."

"We just took out the toys," Dick explained hastily as they clustered about the table.

Conscious of all eyes upon her, Edna minced across the room and took a big cake box from the highest shelf. She bore it proudly to the table, pausing for a dramatic moment before she lifted the lid and placed the cake on the table. Three layers high, it was covered with chocolate frosting and decorated with stars and stripes all red and white and blue! A tribute to Washington on his birthday.

Somehow Jackie managed two big pieces. Mim, who ate slowly and daintily, had time for only one. But Sam and Dick ate three apiece and so did the twins. As

Jackie picked the last crumbs off her pretty blue and white plate, she thought again of the paper tucked deep inside her blouse, the paper for which she had paid so high a sum.

"Thank you very much," she began pushing back from the table, "but we'll have to go now."

Sam and Dick looked up surprised, but she gave them a warning wink and they, too, stood up. So did Mim, reluctantly.

One by one they shook hands with Mrs. Mason, thanked her for the party, and promised to come back. At the door Sam and Dick lifted the boxes over the threshold into the living room.

Mrs. Mason watched them silently, her eyes watery, her lips set in a sad tight smile. Jackie glanced at her uncomfortably. Then, giving the boys a shove, she hurried them across the porch, taking her questionable prize safely out of Edna's reach.

Miriam alone lingered behind. "I'll be along soon," she called after them. "I just must see how Edna looks in my red wool dress." Miriam had never noticed the fight and the paper for which Jackie must pay so high a price.

Once again the Ghostly Trio were alone. Out of sight of the house the boys stopped and turned toward Jackie. They didn't speak, but their eyes asked why she had hurried them away so soon.

"Yes, why?" thought Jackie. She put her hand to her breast. "It can't be anything," she told herself sternly. Yet she couldn't stop the delicious excitement or the horrid apprehension that tingled through her body.

Under the pines the rain was scarcely noticeable as it fell in a soft mist on the boys' expectant faces. Jackie opened her coat and dug her hand deep into her blouse. It closed over the paper.

"It's—it's probably nothing," she declared, trying to keep her hopes from soaring as she pulled it out into the open.

Sam and Dick pressed close, as Jackie, with hands that shook, tenderly smoothed out her bit of trash. It was old and yellowed and lined with creases. In the dim light under the pines, the faded penciled figures were barely visible:

$$2.49$$
$$3.26$$
$$1.98$$
$$\overline{4.56}$$
$$\overline{\$12.29}$$

"Oh." Jackie stared miserably at the long, disappointing column. "I might have known."

"You're nuts," Dick announced without sympathy.

But Sam had dropped to his knees in front of her. His eyes bulging, he gaped at the other side of the paper.

"Turn it over," he whispered huskily.

Jackie turned.

16. THE REWARD

THROUGH the mistlike rain three pairs of eyes strained, three foreheads puckered, three mouths silently formed the words of the dulled, yet bold, old-fashioned writing:

. . . arriv'd at Philadelphia Fryday in good health tho something fatigued with the Journey.

I take this opportunity to offer most unfeigned thanks for your hearty demonstrations of Friendship and Hospitality. Please to make my Compliments agreeable to Mrs. King who has my most sincere and hearty wishes for every thing.

I am, Sir, Yr. most Obedt. and most Humble Servt.

G° Washington

"Gee willigers!" Jackie's squeal penetrated to the topmost branches of the pines. With an effort she sobered her radiant face. "Sam," she whispered, "do you think it really is?"

Sam opened his mouth but no words came. His eyes wide, he stared at her helplessly, nodding his head.

"Put it away before it gets wet," Dick advised nervously.

Scarcely daring to touch it now, Jackie folded the paper with trembling fingers before laying it carefully under her blouse, flat against her rapidly beating heart.

In the soft mist that filtered through the pine boughs the Ghostly Trio stared dumbly at each other, the weight of their discovery almost too huge for them to bear.

"The—the—treasure," Jackie stammered. "Do—do you think it really is?"

Sam nodded. "But how can we be sure?" For all his thinking, he never had thought things out this far.

"Maybe—" Jackie spoke reluctantly. It was their secret, the Ghostly Trio's secret. But there were times when grown-up advice was necessary and this seemed one of them. "Maybe Dr. Miland would know. He's always talking history."

"Dr. Miland. That's the ticket!" Without waiting for the others to decide, Dick went bounding away down the slope and through the meadow.

Fifteen minutes later, red-faced and breathless, the three dashed into the drugstore.

"Doc, Doc, can we see you?" Dick gasped between pants.

Dr. Miland smiled down at the three excited faces. "See me?" Puzzled, he scratched his shiny bald head. "Oh, you mean in private?" He winked.

They nodded speechless as the druggist led them down a narrow dark hall into his sitting room at the back of the store. With a sigh he let himself down into the only easy chair, lit a pipe, stretched out his short fat legs, and waited for them to begin.

Slowly, very slowly, Jackie drew out the precious paper and handed it to Dr. Miland.

The druggist accepted the letter, his face serious and grave. But it was easy to see that he was trying not to smile. That he was just playing up to them the way grownups sometimes did.

But as he read, he started in his chair, sank back with a long surprised gasp, and read again. Without a whisper, without a sound, the Ghostly Trio watched, their hearts pounding.

At last Dr. Miland pushed his glasses up on his round forehead and turned to look at them. His dark eyes met theirs with a flash of excitement. They knew now they had not bothered him for nothing.

"Where did you get this?" he asked sharply.

"Oh, we just found it," Jackie answered evasively.

"Is it the real thing?" cried Dick, not once doubting that it was.

"Mustn't jump at conclusions," the druggist warned, pointing a chubby finger at Dick.

On a sudden inspiration he bounced lightly to his feet and went across the room to the bookshelves that lined the wall. "Anything to do with history, just come to me," he muttered, his eyes traveling along the rows of dusty, unused volumes.

"Ah." With a little sigh he pulled out an old textbook and settled again in his chair.

The Trio gathered close, leaning over his shoulder, breathing down his neck. Dr. Miland flicked rapidly through the pages. Then, coming to an engraving, he opened the book wide and laid their letter gently down on the opposite page.

Jackie pressed still closer. The book was open at a familiar picture. George Washington, white-wigged, with thin serious mouth and dark penetrating eyes, stared back at her from the printed page. Beneath the portrait was a facsimile of his signature. *G° Washington.* The period was a circle above the line, just like a little "o." The "t" was crossed with a swirling loop. Like Dr. Miland, the Trio looked from letter to book, from book to letter.

"It's the same. Boy, oh boy, it's the same." Jackie went up and down like a Pogo stick.

"We can sell it, we'll be rich." Dick was jumping too.

"If I'd only known they had his signature in a book," Sammy sighed, "it would have saved us lots of time."

"Now look," Dr. Miland spoke gravely, controlling the emotion in his voice. "I'm your friend. There are certain things I've got to know if I'm going to help you."

The Trio nodded uneasily and settled themselves in a stiff row on the high backless couch.

"Edna was brushing out his clothes, Old Mason's I mean, and that's how I found—"

Jackie started at the end, but the others took up the threads and went back. Dr. Miland listened thoughtfully, nodding his head from time to time to show he understood.

"You're pretty smart, aren't you?" he commented when they'd finished.

"Yes, sir," Dick answered without modesty. "Now what about that letter? Is it—is it—er—"

"Genuine?" Sam helped out.

"That's for the experts to decide. But I think it must be," Dr. Miland answered turning the letter over and studying it first from one angle, then from another. "The ink is awful faded as if it might have been lying out in the light, and most of the wrinkles won't ever come out. Then there's all those figures on the back. Some of 'em show right through. They don't help the value much."

"Oh," Jackie let out a low disappointed groan.

"But, just the same," the druggist went on cheerfully, "I wouldn't be surprised if the Kingsville Historical Association would give a good sum for it. If not, I could take it to the city the end of the week. Want to get all we can for it."

"Oh," the couch springs squeaked with the joy of Dick's bouncing. "Then maybe we can buy a tent."

"And toys for the Masons," Sam added. "Oh, brother, did they like my top!"

"Yes," Dr. Miland agreed soberly. "The Masons could use toys, and other things still more. In Mr. King's will Old Mason was left only that tiny tenant's house and the wood lot on the knoll. No one thought how he would earn enough to feed his son's widow and children he had always supported, let alone buy them toys." Dr. Miland sighed and wiped his forehead before he went on.

"The old man never had done any other kind of work. Not many people have places big enough to need caretakers these days. He wasn't a bad man. Perhaps he wasn't very smart. Never had a chance to go to high school like you kids today. They've had it tough."

"Oh," said Jackie. She was thinking of Edna. It must have been tough for her too.

"We've tried to keep it quiet so people would forget," the druggist went on. "Everybody liked Old Mason but some like to gossip, especially about others' misfortunes. And when the family ran off with him like that half an hour before the officers came with the warrant, it really set tongues buzzing."

"Oh," said Jackie, "that's about what we figured happened."

"Makes it hard for the old man," Mr. Miland shook his head sadly, "particularly now he'll be looking for a job. That's why I told you to stay away from that house. Just didn't seem right to have anyone snooping around. But—" he broke off and cast a loving look at the letter in his lap.

"Yikes!" Suddenly ill at ease, Dick stood up. "We better buy those suckers quick and pay Edna off." His face, a moment ago so happy, now wore a decidedly worried look.

"We'll sure buy her big ones, eh?" he cried gaily. His voice was strident, the gaiety false.

"Y-y-yes." Jackie's forehead clouded. She ran her tongue thoughtfully over her teeth, feeling the hard smooth binding of her brace.

"Come on, Jackie." Dick shifted in the doorway. "Don't you think we better buy them?" That wasn't like Dick, asking advice, particularly Jackie's.

"N-no," Jackie answered gravely. "I think that Edna better do without them."

"But the letter," Dick protested. "We gotta pay for it, don't we? Or it wouldn't be ours!"

"I wonder if it should be." Jackie looked questioningly at Sam, but his eyes avoided hers. Dr. Miland studied the letter as if he had forgotten them.

"It was only a scrap to them." Dick's voice was loud, the way it often got when he was uncertain or confused. "We could help them, too."

"I think," Sam broke his long brooding silence, "that they would rather help themselves. I think the letter should be theirs."

"I—I think so too." Jackie's face brightened as if a great weight had been lifted from her heart. But again she turned to Dick for the last word, the way she always did.

For a long moment of indecision Dick shuffled in the doorway.

"All right," he said at last, "if that's the way you feel." His voice was gloomy, but the worried look on his face had unaccountably changed to a happy one. He sat down again beside Jackie and Sam.

"But," Dr. Miland looked up from the letter as if he had been listening all the time and knew the decision they had reached. "But—"

He was interrupted by a sudden knock at the door, and a big man with a wind-burned face came into the room. It was Mr. Blake from the Wildwood Construction Company.

"That blasted night watchman didn't show up again. I've got to have a new one for Wildwood. Thought you might know of someone locally, Doc," he bellowed in his big outdoor voice.

"A night watchman?" Jackie asked. "Isn't that something like a caretaker?"

"Why yes, Reds," Mr. Blake grinned. "Now that you mention it. Except a watchman only works a shift."

"How about Old Mason?" Jackie whispered to the druggist. She felt very bold and grown up and responsible.

"You say he's coming home tomorrow?"

Jackie nodded solemnly, but inside she was all but bursting with pride and pleasure.

"There's the man for you, Blake. Old John Mason from back on the knoll." Dr. Miland stood up as if to dismiss his visitor. "I'll send him around to talk to you."

"Oh, you mean the late Mr. King's caretaker? So he got his parole!"

The Trio exchanged quick glances. Then they had been right about Mason. In spite of running away, he must have been caught and tried and sentenced. But now he was free again to come home to the Mystery House and Edna and the twins.

"Sure," Mr. Blake went on. "I know about him. Like to help him out. Well, so long and thanks for the tip, Reds." He laughed uproariously, tipped his hat which he hadn't bothered to remove, and disappeared into the hall.

"Of course," Dr. Miland turned again to the Trio, his voice brusque and businesslike, "as agents selling the letter you people will be entitled to a commission."

"Agents? Commission?" Dick scratched his head.

"Agents are people who sell things for other people," Sam explained.

"And commission, that's the part of the money the agents get for their trouble." Exploding with joy and excitement Jackie began to bounce.

"I don't suppose it will be very much," the druggist warned.

"It depends on what we can finally get for the letter. But—" His eyes sparkled at them. "Just what do you kids especially want?"

"Yikes!" Dick explained. "Ah—er—ah—" It seemed as if there were a hundred things he was always wanting. But now it was hard to think of things he didn't have.

"We've already got bikes," said Jackie. A bike was the most important thing a boy or girl could own.

"Something that could be for all of you," Dr. Miland suggested. "Something you could use together."

"I'd like books," said Sammy, "but I don't think—"

"How about that tent?" Dick interrupted. "We could pitch it by the lake."

"Oh, the lake," said Jackie remembering her island. "You know what I'd like most of all?"

"What?" the boys asked in unison.

Jackie only shook her head. "It's no good. We couldn't even use one."

"Tell us anyway," prompted Dr. Miland.

"A boat," Jackie sighed. "But boating's forbidden on the lake."

"Well, there's a possibility." Dr. Miland wiped his face

in his characteristic manner. "But I guess you kids wouldn't have heard."

"Heard what?" cried Dick.

"There's talk of turning Lake Kingsville into a recreational area. It's to come up at town meeting next week." Dr. Miland stood up and so did the Trio, for once too overwhelmed for comment.

"Unless the idea's voted down," the druggist continued as he led the way to the door and solemnly shook hands with each of them, "I can assure you that boating and swimming will not be frowned upon."

Leaving the precious letter for Dr. Miland to lock in his safe, the three set out exultantly for home. As they reached the top of the hill the setting sun came through the rain clouds in the west, its glow reflected in the distant water of the lake.

A great happiness filled Jackie. A happiness too big for casual talk or even singing. Not even in those far-off days when she was very small could she remember feeling quite like this. Glancing sideways at Sam's round beaming face and Dick's quick excited grin, she knew they felt it too.

It was not only because spring was on the way. Not only because the lake might be truly theirs at last with maybe even a boat to go with it. There was something more besides. All at once Jackie knew that if they had kept the letter for themselves, they never could have felt as wonderful as this.